BEING
HENRY
DAVID

cal armistead

ALBERT WHITMAN & COMPANY
CHICAGO, ILLINOIS

Armistead, Cal.
Being Henry David / by Cal Armistead.
p. cm.
Summary: "Seventeen-year-old 'Hank,' who can't remember his identity,
finds himself in Penn Station with a copy of Thoreau's *Walden* as his
only possession and must figure out where he's from and why he ran away."
—Provided by publisher.
ISBN 978-0-8075-0615-8 (hardcover)
[1. Amnesia—Fiction. 2. Street children—Fiction. 3. Thoreau, Henry David.
Walden—Fiction. 4. Runaways—Fiction. 5. Family problems—Fiction.
6. Guilt—Fiction. 7. New York (N.Y.)—Fiction. 8. Concord (Mass.)—Fiction.]
I. Title.
PZ7.A7248Bei 2013
[Fic]—dc23
2012017377

The design is by Nick Tiemersma.
Cover images courtesy of Veer.

For more information about Albert Whitman & Company,
visit our web site at www.albertwhitman.com.

To T-4.

For all the reasons.

1

THE LAST THING I REMEMBER IS NOW.

Now, coming at me with heart-pounding fists. My eyes shoot open, and there is too much. Of everything. Blurred figures, moving. White lights. Muffled waves of sound. Voices. Music. Chaos.

"You gonna eat that?"

A noise at my ear. I turn. Smear of a face, too close. Its mouth moves, can't make sense of the words. Close my eyes, rub hard. Sore and gritty. I open them. Blink and blink. Senses snap into focus.

Everything in this place is washed of color. Tile on the floor is gray and white. Pumped-in classical music, way too loud. Crazy violins. Nothing makes sense.

"You gonna eat that?"

A fat man stares into my face. Long tangled hair, streaked gray, bushy beard. Eyes all watery and blood-shot. I sit on the floor leaning against a wall, the man sits next to me, gray football jersey and dirty blue sweat-pants. Stinking of unwashed body and stale tobacco, with crusty bits of food in his beard.

A loudspeaker crackle jolts me and a bored woman's voice says, "Final call, nonstop service, track twelve, all aboard." Over the shaggy man's head, a huge sign hangs from the ceiling, black with white letters and numbers that flip and change next to names: Trenton; Washington DC; Niagara Falls; Boston.

Cities. They are cities. I understand that much at least. People are here to go to the cities on the sign. I don't have a backpack or suitcase, but I figure I'm a traveler too. Why else would I be here?

All I understand is that I was sleeping, and now I am awake. So why don't I remember anything that came before the sleeping?

The man speaks again, and I blink hard. Am I going to eat *what*? I look around, notice my own muddy gray sneakers on big feet. Faded blue jeans, ripped at the knee, black T-shirt, and a gray hooded sweatshirt. I don't remember putting on these clothes or walking in mud.

I reach up to scratch my head and feel a sharp, stinging

pain. When I pull my hand away, there's blood on my fingertips. I touch again, more gently this time. Just under my hairline, there's a huge lump with a crusty scab that I just scratched off. Luckily it's not bleeding much, so I wipe the blood on my jeans like it doesn't matter. But my eyes prickle and burn. All I want is to get out of this place and go home.

Searching my brain for what home means, I find a white blank space. Where, what, is *home*?

I fumble in my pockets for an ID. There's a crumpled ten dollar bill in a front pocket, nothing else. I think I'm old enough to have a driver's license and for a second, I see myself behind the wheel of a car. But then that shred of memory shuts down on me, hard, like a slammed door echoing down a long hallway.

"Hey! You gonna eat that?" The guy sounds angry now, furry black eyebrows crunched together.

I search around me again on the tile floor. If I find anything to eat, I'll gladly give it to this annoying dude, make him go away so I can think. But the only thing I find is a green paperback book, under my right leg. I lift up the book, in case he thinks I'm hiding food under it. Nothing.

I shrug, book still in my hand. "No food." My voice is a low, unfamiliar croak.

His bloodshot eyes never blink and never leave the book. Testing him, I lift it a few inches, shift it to the left, the right, set it back on the floor next to me. His zombie gaze drifts left, right, and down, following the book.

What the hell? I squint down to scan the title, but the next thing I know, a huge paw with grimy fingernails snatches the book away. With surprising speed for a guy his size, the man hauls himself to his feet and lumbers away from me, book pressed against his beard, into a sea of people who apparently got off a train all at once.

"Hey!" I shout after him. For one confused moment, I'm too stunned to move. Then I scramble to my feet and put these long legs to work, chasing after what is my only possession in this world as far as I know.

The big guy is a pro at dodging through people and briefcases and duffel bags and wheeled suitcases. Me, not so much. I run smack into a tall guy in a black raincoat and he drops a leather notebook on the floor.

"Dammit, kid," he shouts at me. Papers fly all over. He looks like he wants to punch me. I help him pick up the papers, apologizing constantly, pushing them into his hands while he murmurs, "yeah, whatever, just get away from me." I swing around to search for the guy who stole my book and he's gone.

I push through the crowd—*sorry, excuse me, sorry*—and finally spot him by the men's room. He's on the floor, leaning against the gray wall with his thick, stubby legs stretched out in front of him, hunkered down over the book—my book—turning pages and concentrating, like he's looking for something. Then he grabs the corner of one of the pages from the middle of the book and rips it out.

Before I can react, he takes the torn-out page, crumples it into a ball, stuffs the whole thing into his mouth, and starts chewing. With a black smudged pinky extended, he tears out another one. I stare in disbelief as he swallows that page, and chomps down on another.

"Give me the book." My voice is a pretty impressive growl, but all he does is glare, sheltering the book with his wide body as he rips out another random page and stuffs it into his mouth.

Somebody else might have given up, just walked away and bought himself another damn book. But somebody else didn't just appear out of nowhere in a train station with no ID or luggage. No memory, not even a name. Just a book. A book that might carry a clue, like maybe the name of its owner (me) scrawled inside the front cover. Or a receipt from a hometown grocery store stuffed between its pages. Or a ticket home. I have to know, have to get that book back.

So I reach right under the big dude's reeking armpit, and grab the book. He holds it tight with his pudgy fingers and makes a puffing noise, fighting me off. He's strong and stubborn, I'll give him that. We wrestle, both of us grunting and pulling. His tobacco breath is a toxic cloud and his armpits smell like onion soup gone bad, but I refuse to give up. Then, out of nowhere, he lets out this strange bellow, like a walrus at the zoo. I can actually feel the sound vibrations travel through my hands, up both arms, and into my chest. He roars again and pulls at the book.

"Let *go!*" I shout and yank back.

"Okay, you two, break it up, hear? Step away, now."

An iron hand clamps around my upper arm, and I whirl around to see a couple of uniformed cops peering down at us. One of them, a redheaded guy with a baby face, has my arm. At the sight of the blue uniform, I have an instinctive urge to pull my arm away and bolt. But I force myself to freeze, as if avoiding any sudden movements will keep me safe.

"What's going on here?" asks the other cop, a dark-skinned guy, taller and thinner than his partner. His face looks young, but he has a thick gray mustache, so I figure he's at least in his forties.

When I glance at his badge and the navy blue POLICE cap on his head, a strange terror grips my gut. I swallow hard and lick my dry lips before I can speak. "My book," I say, and I stand up, glad to pull away from Red the cop and the stench of the big man. "He stole my book, and he's…" I gesture helplessly, and the three of us look down at him. "He's eating it."

The big man, still chewing on paper and drooling into his beard, glances at each of us and grins.

"Frankie, did you take this boy's book?" The gray mustached cop asks patiently, like he's talking to a little kid.

Frankie shakes his massive head and swallows. "Mine."

Red puts his hands on his hips. "Sorry, kid," he says to me. "Frankie here has some sort of mental issue that makes him eat weird stuff. I've seen him eat cigarette butts and string before."

"He ate an entire bar of soap once," Mustache Cop adds, nodding. "I watched him."

We all stare at Frankie again like he's a science experiment, and he gives us this huge smile.

"Anyway, kid, though I tend to believe you, it's your word against Frankie's. He says it's his, you say it yours." The police radio on his shoulder crackles, and he ignores it.

Anger boils up inside my chest. They can't let this guy keep my book. They can't.

"But tell you what," says Red. "I have an idea. Frankie, hand over the book."

Frankie stuffs one more page into his mouth, then shrugs and gives him the book. That easy. The cop hides it behind his back.

"Okay. The first one of you to give me the correct title and author of this book is the rightful owner and shall be reunited with his property." He looks each of us in the eye to prolong the suspense, and then says: "*Go.*"

My palms start sweating. I'd only gotten one quick peek at the title before Frankie swiped the book. If I'd been reading the book before I fell asleep, I remember nothing about it now. I'm embarrassed to feel tears of frustration sting the backs of my eyeballs. But then I see the green cover in my head, the picture of a lake. This is weird, but it's like I know this place. I can smell the water and hear the birds. And then I see the title in my head, as if the words were stamped on the inside of my eyelids.

"It's *Walden*," I say, all in a rush.

Red nods. "And the author? For extra credit?" He chuckles. The guy is getting a real charge out of himself.

"Aw, give the kid the break," Mustache Cop says.

"No, it's okay," I say because I see it again, that picture in my head. "Henry David Thoreau, right?"

"Yes, indeed. Henry David Thoreau," Mustache Cop says, nodding his head adamantly. Then he clears his throat and takes a dramatic stance. "'I went into the woods because I wanted to live deliberately. I wanted to live deep and suck out all the marrow of life.'" Grinning, he nods at us, all proud of himself. "See there? See? That's from the book. I memorized that stuff way back in high school." He taps his forehead. "Like a steel trap."

"Whatever," I mumble, but neither of them seems to hear. This guy can remember a high school English assignment word-for-word and I don't even know my own name. I consider telling the cops that I'm lost and can't remember who I am. Maybe they can help me. But there's that thing in my chest like a brick wall that says this would be a terrible idea. Some fuzzy instinct tells me it's not safe to go to the police. Fuzzy instinct isn't much to go on, but it's all I have. I decide to trust it.

Red stares at his partner for a second. "Suck out the marrow? Is that what you said? Now that's just disgusting."

Mustache Cop just shakes his head and smiles. He has a nice smile, straight white teeth. "Seize the day, young man. *Carpe diem.* That's what Thoreau was talking about."

"Uh. Excuse me? Officers?" I say politely. They turn

blank eyes at me, as though they've forgotten I'm still here. "Can I have my book?"

"What? Oh yeah, sure." Red hands me the book.

"*Walden* by Henry David Thoreau," Mustache Cop says again, poking a finger at the name on the cover. "Now that guy knew what he was talking about. If we all lived like him, the world would be a better place."

"Not if it means eating marrow and whatnot." His partner shakes his head and his chubby red cheeks wiggle. "That's just sick."

The two transit cops walk off arguing, and I relax, relieved to see them go.

I examine the cover of the book, try to wipe off Frankie's grimy fingerprints and a few smudges of dark chewing tobacco drool with the sleeve of my sweatshirt. Then I hold it shut with both hands, tight, like I'm protecting all those pages and words and punctuation; all mine.

I glare at Frankie, but he's not even looking in my direction. Instead, he's staring at the people who hustle by where he sits on the floor, bloodshot eyes scanning them for something edible, studying what they hold in their hands or have tucked under their arms.

His gaze locks onto a woman holding a pair of leather gloves, and then a little girl clutching a purple stuffed elephant.

"You gonna eat that?"

They rush past, looking alarmed.

I search for a chair so I can sit and flip through the book, but the only ones available are in a special area for people with train tickets. So I find a quiet corner and sit on the floor again, desperate to know the clues that *Walden* by Henry David Thoreau might hold. Whoever he is. And whoever I am.

2

YEAH, I LOOKED THROUGH THAT DAMN BOOK. I SAT FOR A good twenty minutes and flipped through every single page. There was nothing. Not a train ticket, not a receipt, not a name. Nothing.

So. What now? Burying my face in my hands, I fight an urge to rock back and forth, crying like some lost little kid. Instead, I'm distracted by the feel of soft stubble on my chin. Not much of a beard, but apparently enough to shave. My fingers explore my cheeks, nose, eyelids, and ears like a blind person. I don't even know what I look like yet. Would I know me if I saw me? Got to find a mirror.

As soon as I step into the men's room, the strong smell of piss and disinfectant stings the inside of my nose, and some guy is puking in one of the stalls. Ignoring this, I freeze in front of the mirror. I blink, and the guy in the mirror blinks back. Stuffing *Walden* into the back waistband of my jeans to get it out of the way, I lean in to stare at the stranger. Damp hair, black and straight. Messy. I rake my fingers through it. Eyes light, maybe gray. He's tall and lanky, but his shoulders—*my* shoulders—are wide and I look strong. That's something anyway.

"Hey, ugly," comes a voice. There's a skinny kid leaning against the wall by the urinals, one boot up against the concrete, dirty blond hair falling into his eyes. His clothes look like they could use a washing. Or better yet, a Dumpster.

"Hey, asswipe," I say back. Among the things I've just learned about the guy in the mirror are: One, I could easily take this loser. And two, I'm no rock star, but I'm definitely not ugly.

The kid's mouth twists to one side, and his eyes blaze. I just want to be left alone. But if he wants to start something, okay then. I'll fight him. My hands curl into fists as I wait for him to make the first move.

"Yeah? Wipe your own ugly ass," he hisses. He takes three steps toward me, eyes never leaving mine. We stare into each other's faces, neither giving any ground, not one centimeter, not one twitch of surrender. Then before I can react, he pushes me forward with hard palms, trying to slam me against the concrete wall. I barely waver.

"That was lame," I say.

He gets close, peers into my face, his mouth a tight line of aggression. I stare back, not flinching, not even blinking.

Then he smiles. He laughs and slaps me on the shoulder and I'm so tensed up, I almost react with a fist to his jaw, except that his attitude seems friendly. Weirdly friendly.

"I'm Jack," he says. "Don't ask for a last name, because I don't have one." He crosses his arms across his chest and smiles at me, and I realize that I've passed some kind of test. My fist relaxes, finger by finger, joint by joint.

The puking guy stumbles out of the stall to shuffle toward the sinks, and Jack and I give him plenty of room. His eyes are bloodshot, cheeks caved in like a decaying jack-o'-lantern, his flannel shirt grimy. His glassy eyes drift toward me, and he gives me a slow smile. The few teeth he has left in his mouth are black nubs.

"Later, boys," he says. He lurches out the door.

Jack ignores him. "So who the hell are you?" he asks me.

Good question. Who the hell *am* I? I clear my throat, adjust my jeans to buy some time. And I feel the bulk of the paperback book stuffed into the waistband. A picture of the cover swims into my mind again. I see the lake, the trees. Then the title and the author's name.

"Henry," I blurt out. "Henry David."

Jack pauses, and for a second I think he's going to call me on it. I probably didn't say it with enough conviction. *Henry. Henry David.* Next time, I'll do better.

"Henry," he says doubtfully, trying it out. "You don't look like a Henry. I'll call you Hank." And just like that, I become Hank. "So, Hank, I think it's about time for a midnight snack. You got any money?"

I shrug. "A little."

"Good. You can buy us some food."

I narrow my eyes. This guy has some balls. "Why don't you buy us some food? Since it was your idea and all."

"Relax, Hank. Give me something, and I'll give you something. Like maybe a warm place to sleep tonight. Don't you think that's worth the price of a hamburger, for chrissake?"

❦

The ten dollars in my pocket isn't a lot of cash, but it's

enough to buy Jack and me sodas and two cheeseburgers each at a fast food place in the terminal. Judging by the way he stuffs the first burger into his mouth and lets the ketchup dribble down his chin, he's hungrier than I am or a slob. Or both.

"So what are you running away from, Hank?"

I pull a pickle out of my burger and pop it into my mouth. I can't remember food ever tasting so good. But then, I can't actually remember eating anything before this.

"What makes you think I'm running?"

Jack smirks and swipes at his chin with a paper napkin. "You're hiding out at Penn Station. Any second, you look like you could either bust into tears or stab a guy in the neck. It's *the look*."

"*The look*." I echo.

"Yeah, the one you get when you're a runaway, especially at the beginning."

"I don't know what you're talking about." I take a huge gulp of soda to wash down the lump in my throat.

"Yeah, you do. You're scared shitless, but you still figure being on the streets is better than being at home." Jack stuffs another bite of cheeseburger into his mouth and pokes a finger at my chest. "You can't bullshit me, 'cause I'm the same as you," he says with his mouth full.

I'm nothing like you, I want to tell him, taking in his

filthy clothes and the dark smudges under his eyes from dirt or lack of sleep. But what if I *am* a runaway, and things were so terrible where I came from, I blocked them from my memory? My fingers seek out that sore spot on my head under my hair, with its dried blood and goose-egg lump. What happened to me?

"I've heard all the stories. Let me guess yours." He looks me up and down. "Don't tell me. You're a foster kid who aged out of the system."

I shrug, not sure what else to do.

"Wait, wait, I got it," Jack says. "You did something, didn't you?"

The lump on my head begins to throb.

"Ah, we're getting close," Jack crows. "What'd you do, break into a house? Steal a car?"

Sweat breaks out on my upper lip.

"Oh, I know. Maybe you killed somebody."

He laughs after he says *maybe you killed somebody*, loving his own crazy joke, and I try to join in, but my face is frozen. My pulse hammers in my ears and something dark lurches in my chest like a beast waking from a deep sleep. A wave of dizziness breaks over me and I grip the edge of the table so I won't fall off the chair.

"Dude, you okay?" Jack's thin face drifts in and out of focus.

A trickle of sweat trails between my shoulder blades. I wipe my upper lip with the back of a shaky hand. "Yeah. Yeah, I'm okay."

"You looked like you were about to have a seizure or something," Jacks says. "You one of those epileptics?"

I take deep breaths, needing hits of oxygen. "Just dizzy, that's all." My mouth is desert-dry, so I grab my soda and gulp it down. Slowly, I feel my heart and breathing return to normal, and I sense the black thing in my chest (what the hell was that?) hunker down and go quiet.

Jack squints at me, but then jerks to attention like a deer smelling a predator, turning toward the entrance of the restaurant. The two transit cops I met earlier are standing there. Their glances sweep the room and lock in on us. They start toward us, and Jack freezes. Red hitches up his pants over his belly.

"You back again, Jack?" asks the cop with the mustache. He smiles, but the grin looks more menacing than friendly.

Jack slouches down in his chair. "Just enjoying a delicious meal, officer, like any other paying customer. No law against that, is there?"

"No, but if you overstay your welcome, we'll have another conversation. Understand?"

Jack nods, his eyes sleepy. "I most certainly do, officer."

Mustache Cop's gaze trails over to me. "You enjoying that book, kid? You seizing the day?"

"Yes, sir."

"Hmm. Yeah, I can see that. Just watch yourself with Jack here. You look like a good kid, and I don't want his influence rubbing off on you." His eyes drill into mine, like he's trying to extract something.

"Yes, sir." I say again. Lame.

Finally, without another word to us, the cops finish surveying the restaurant, then seeming satisfied, they leave, radios crackling in their wake.

"I hate those guys," Jack murmurs to me. "They seem to like you, though. Must be the preppy kid look you've got going on. And those running shoes. Bet they cost you like two hundred bucks."

I examine my innocent gray sneakers as if they hold some story they can tell me about myself. Jack looks too.

"Is that why you talked to me?" I ask him. "You think I'm some rich kid?"

"Not at all," Jack says, his blues eyes all wide. "I talked to you because I could see you were lost and needed a friend." He stands up and tucks the second cheeseburger in the pocket of his green army jacket. "Let's go. I got a place where we can crash for a couple hours."

Jack starts walking toward an exit and I stay frozen in my seat, not knowing what to do. When he notices I'm not following, he turns and stares at me, annoyed.

"Look, it's past midnight in New York City, Hank. You really want to be here at Penn Station all alone with the crazies?"

Somebody else might have said, *you go ahead, I'll stay here*. Somebody else might have trusted his gut, which was telling me Jack could only lead me to trouble. But I'm not somebody else, and I don't have a better plan. Jack has decided to be my friend, and that's all I've got. So I go with him.

Out on the street, the sounds, smells, and lights of the city at night crash over me like a wave. Stale car exhaust. Glaring artificial light. Horns honk, people shout, and from far away a car alarm drones. The city itself is like some kind of huge, restless, living organism.

Jack leads me through the charged air, turning left down one street, then another. The place is alive with people and noise, even though it's past midnight. Taxicabs clatter by and honk for no apparent reason. A guy in a dirty black jacket sits on a milk crate playing an acoustic guitar, and I stop to watch his fingers fly across the frets, his right hand picking and strumming. A woman drops a dollar bill into his open guitar case. Jack comes back and grabs my arm just as I empty out the coins in my pocket.

"What are you doing?" he asks.

"I don't know." I shrug. "He was really good."

In spite of the bombardment of noises and smells, I memorize every turn, including two more lefts onto smaller streets, just in case I need to find my way back to the train station.

"Where you taking me?" I say at last.

"Relax, already. We're almost there," Jack says.

One more turn, and we walk down a narrow alley littered with scraps of wood and rusty pipes. A light shines down onto a big green Dumpster at its end.

"Home sweet home," says Jack.

"What, you live in a Dumpster?"

"Behind it, prep boy. They're doing renovations on the second floor, so it's full of construction stuff. You wouldn't believe what they throw away."

Behind the Dumpster, I see a lean-to shack made of broken slabs of wood and sheets of plastic, propped up against the brick wall like a crooked little fairy tale house.

Jack goes over to the shack and pounds on a slab of

cracked drywall that makes the roof. Colored beads hang from the front of the shack. Apparently somebody tried to decorate. "Hey, Nessa, you home?"

There's a rustling inside the shack, and a girl emerges from behind a ragged patchwork quilt serving as a door. Her hair is long and black, and she has heavy makeup smeared around her pale eyes.

"Hey, Jack," Nessa slurs, either sleepy or wasted.

"How'd it go tonight?"

Nessa shakes her head and tugs at her huge gray sweatshirt. "Not so good." Her legs are skinny, bird legs in thick black tights. She's probably fourteen or fifteen years old, but even with all that makeup, she looks like a little girl. She catches a glimpse of me, hovering there behind Jack.

"Who are you?" she asks, looking me over with husky-dog blue eyes.

"I'm Hank."

"Cool. You're cute," she says and gives me this sweet smile.

Jack ducks into the shack, leaving Nessa and me standing there. I wish I knew how to turn the volume down on the sadness in this girl's eyes. I wish I could take her out of this dark, smelly alley and tuck her away someplace safe.

"Uh, thanks," is all I can think of to say. "So are you."
Brilliant.

Jack comes out carrying two blankets and a pack of cigarettes. He offers me a thin wool blanket. It's gray, full of holes and smells like mothballs and piss, but the night is chilly, so I take it, hoping it's not crawling with bugs or something. Wrapped up in the blankets, we lean back against the Dumpster. Nessa nestles between us, and Jack hands her the cheeseburger he saved from our snack at the terminal.

"Aww, thanks, sweetie," she says. "I'm starving."

"Hank bought it."

"Then thank *you*, sweetie," she says to me, and I nod as if it were my idea, wishing it was. She chews the first bite with her eyes closed like it's a gourmet meal instead of a cold, greasy burger.

I take the cigarette Jack offers, poke its tip in the flame of his lighter, and puff. Smoke in my lungs feels familiar. I must be a smoker, then. We sit there for a while just smoking together, and something inside me relaxes for the first time.

"Check out the moon," Nessa says.

It takes a moment to see it past the glaring lights of the city, but then, there it is, big and full, glowing orange like an omen. Good or bad? I wish I knew.

I look at Nessa's pretty profile as she tilts her head to look at the sky. "Makes me think of this book I really liked when I was a little kid," she says, her voice quiet. "I think it was called *Goodnight Moon*."

Jack snorts. "Yeah, except out here, it would go something like, 'goodnight junkies, goodnight rats, goodnight Dumpster, goodnight trash.'"

Nessa smiles at him, but her voice is still dreamy. "Remember that book, Hank?"

"Nope," I say.

"You're kidding, right?" Jack says. "Every kid knows that book."

I shake my head and take another drag of the cigarette. "I don't remember."

We smoke in silence for a bit, so quiet I can hear faraway sirens and the crackle of our cigarette paper burning down.

"Mom used to read it out loud," Jack says, still looking up at the moon. "That was before she died and Dad stopped caring whether I went to school or not or whether I was alive or dead. Until the day he came after me with a shovel. Then I was pretty sure he wanted me dead." Jack gives me a sidelong look and this weird smirk. "Whatever. Everybody out here has a story." Jack swipes at his face with the wool blanket. "So what's yours?"

Nessa stands up and stretches. "Leave him alone. Can't you see he doesn't want to talk about it?" She rubs her eyes with fists like a sleepy child, further smearing her makeup. "I gotta sleep. Are you going to stay with us a while, Hank?"

"Maybe a little while," I say, though I have no idea. A part of me wants to stick around, like I have this crazy idea I can protect her. Nessa says good night and disappears into the shack.

"Everybody has a story," Jack says, as if there'd been no interruption in our conversation. "No matter how bad it is, I guarantee I've heard it before."

"I doubt it." I stare up at the moon for a long time. Jack and Nessa have taken me in, the only friends I have on this planet. The night is gentle, holding its breath, and at least for this moment in time I feel safe. So I decide to tell him. "My story is that I can't remember my story."

"Say what?"

"I don't remember anything." I lower my voice. "Not my name, not where I came from. I woke up at the train station a couple hours ago, just before I met you, and that's the first thing I can remember."

"Seriously?" The glow of Jack's cigarette hovers motionless. "You mean, like you've got amnesia?"

"Yeah," I say. "I guess so."

"Wow."

"I mean, I *know* stuff. Like, before I ate it, I knew cheeseburgers tasted good. I know about money and train stations, that I live in the United States of America and speak English. I know general stuff about the world. But I don't remember anything, you know, about myself."

"Hmmm." Jack purses his lips as he contemplates this news. "That is so messed up, dude." Then his face twitches into a smile.

"I know." Recognizing the weirdness of my situation, I smile back. When Jack starts laughing, at first I'm a little pissed, but then his laugh is so damn contagious, I'm laughing too. Something in my chest feels lighter with the laughing. Sharing my secret makes it less scary somehow.

"So Henry David isn't your name."

"Nope." I pull *Walden* out of my waistband and hold it up to show Jack. "I just found this book next to me when I woke up, so I used the name of the guy who wrote it. Other than the clothes I'm wearing, it's the only thing I own. I think it must be a clue."

Jack shrugs and takes a deep drag of his cigarette. "Either that or some random person left it at the train station and you just happened to find it."

My jaw clenches. "No way," I say. "It's a clue."

"Take it easy," he says. "Okay, it's a clue." He stubs out his cigarette on the bottom of his sneaker. "So what are you gonna do? Go on national TV and be Amnesia Boy? The media loves that shit. You'll be famous by dinner-time tomorrow." From far away, we hear a police siren. "Just don't say anything about me," Jack says. "I like to keep a low profile. Way low."

"Yeah, I think I need to do the same."

Maybe you killed somebody.

Keeping a low profile is about the only thing I'm sure of. That, and the fact that I woke up with this book next to me. Therefore, it has to mean something. I touch the cover picture of pine trees at the edge of a lake. That's where I want to be.

"Okay, Hank, or whatever your name is, I need to check in on Nessa and crash for a couple hours. Grab some drywall and make yourself a little shelter. Cool?"

"Cool. I'll be fine."

Jack salutes, then disappears into the shack. He and Nessa whisper for a while, then there are soft sounds that could be laughing or crying. After that, silence.

Staring up at the moon, I try to feel sleepy, but now that I'm alone, my mind is racing and I'm wide awake with my heart hammering against my ribs. There are skittering sounds on the other side of the Dumpster, probably rats. The wind shifts, and even though the Dumpster is mostly full of construction trash, I get a strong whiff of rotting food and random nastiness. I pull a huge plank of particle board out of a pile next to the Dumpster, lean it against the back wall of the alley, and huddle underneath like it can keep me safe. I try to stop my hands from shaking.

To calm my twitchy brain, I take a little internal inventory, try to piece together what I know about myself so far. Okay, so I'm a teenage guy, probably somewhere between sixteen and eighteen years old. Hair, black; eyes gray. Not bad-looking either. There was only that quick glance in the men's room mirror, but I know that much. I like burgers and soda, and I might be a smoker, although that cigarette left a weird taste in my mouth that kind of makes me want to gag. I have a bump and a cut above my forehead that stings if I touch it. I get real fidgety around the cops.

And there's a black beast inside me that doesn't want me to know stuff. It guards my memory, clawing at my insides and going for my throat if I get too close. So why did the beast wake up when Jack said, *maybe you killed somebody?* Is that what it won't let me remember?

The black thing in me surges again, and I feel a pounding headache coming on. "Stop," I whisper. "Go away." But it crouches there, waiting to creep closer so it can attack, now while I'm alone and vulnerable. No.

There's a light shining down from the side of the building, bright enough to read by. So I open my book, *Walden* by Henry David Thoreau, and that's what I do.

This Thoreau guy wrote it in the mid-1800s, so the writing is a little weird for me at first. I have to read some paragraphs over a few times to figure out what he's trying to say. But then I start to get into it.

Walden, as it turns out, is named after some pond in the woods in a town called Concord, Massachusetts. Henry David Thoreau was in his late twenties when he went there to get away from the world and live alone in a little cabin for a couple years. He listened to the birds, walked around the pond, and just thought about stuff. Living off the grid, whatever grid there was in 1845.

Instead of the stink of the alley and the echo of sirens and honking taxicabs, while I'm reading the book it's actually like there's fresh air rustling leaves in a tree over my head. I hear the water and birds singing. Somehow, I know this place in Henry's book. I can remember being outside like that, in the woods, near a lake. It's familiar in a way I feel to my bones. It's the closest feeling so far to home.

3

"JACK, YOU SON OF A BITCH. GET OUT HERE!"

I lurch awake, and for a long blank moment I have no idea where I am or what woke me up. *Walden* lies next to me on the ground, where it fell when I went to sleep. There's a good dream lingering behind my eyes and I grasp at it, but it vanishes before I can remember. My heart sinks when I realize where I am. The alley looks even dirtier and more depressing in the first white light of morning.

Then I realize what woke me up. Some guy is shouting in the alley.

"Jack!"

There's a confused rustle inside Nessa's shack, and then Jack emerges, squinting in the morning light, hair sticking up all over his head. He looks past me at someone on the other side of the Dumpster where I can't see.

"What are you doing here?" Jack calls out.

"I want my money back."

I untangle myself from my blanket and peer around the edge of the Dumpster, watching Jack approach some skinny, bent-over guy standing in the alley, hands fisted at his sides. He wears a filthy flannel shirt and his face is like an old man's, all sunken in against his skull. The guy from the train station men's room.

He reaches into the pocket of his shirt, pulls out a plastic baggie, and waves it in Jack's face.

"I don't know what you cut this with, Jack, but it's not right. I want my cash back."

"I don't have the money, Simon. I already gave it to Magpie."

"So get it back from Magpie."

A pause. "I can't do that."

Simon shoves Jack against the Dumpster. Jack's skull slams against the metal, clangs like a muffled bell.

"This is bullshit, Jack."

Jack sits crumpled on the ground, holding the back of his head. I help him to his feet, then turn to face Simon. "Leave him alone," I say. My voice is steady but my heart slams against my ribs like a manic bird in a cage.

Simon cuts bloodshot eyes at me. "Stay out of this." He holds up the baggie and throws it onto Jack's chest. "My money. Now."

The baggie bounces off Jack's chest and lands at my feet.

"I swear, Simon, Magpie said it was pure," Jack says. Leaning hard against the Dumpster, he pulls himself to his feet. "He never cuts, you know that. And I didn't do anything to it."

I pick up the baggie, open it, and peer at the white powder inside, not sure what I'm looking at.

"Do it," Simon says to me.

"Do what?"

"Taste it."

Taste it? The guy is staring at me with his crazy hollow eyes, and it's freaking me out. So I wet my finger, dip it into the powder, and touch it to the end of my tongue.

"It's sweet," I say, surprised. "Like—" I search my memory banks for the thing that reminds me of this taste and consistency. "Powdered sugar or something." And there's another taste too, sharp and bitter.

"Exactly," says Simon, all triumphant. "You cut it with powdered sugar. A lot of it."

"But you tried it," Jack says, desperate. Even his dirty blond hair is trembling. "You said it was fine."

"I was wrong."

"I think *you* did it," somebody says to Simon. And I realize that someone was me. "You cut the stuff so you could sell it and make more profit. And you're trying to blame it on Jack."

Both Simon and Jack stare at me. Simon's left eye twitches. "You're fucking crazy," he says.

"I don't think so."

Simon hesitates. Then he grins at me with those gray-black nubs that used to be teeth. He reaches under his shirt and pulls something out of the back of his belt. A knife. The blade is slender and long, with a black handle. The metal gleams in a shaft of morning light.

"You don't want to do that," I say.

"Actually," says Simon, "I do." He lunges at me, poking the knife at my gut. I dodge and try to kick the knife out of his hand, an unsuccessful karate move. Better just try and pound the crap out of him. I clench my fists and Simon thrusts the knife at me again. This time the blade catches the side of my sweatshirt. There's a ripping sound and I feel a sharp pain in my side. The knife, when Simon pulls it back, is streaked with blood.

Before I can respond, I hear a growl from somewhere behind Simon, and then Jack is jumping on the guy piggyback, wrapping his skinny arms tight around

Simon's neck. Simon bellows, tries to shake Jack off, slices the air with the knife. He manages to break Jack's hold on him, flings him off onto his back, knocking the breath out of him.

From somewhere outside my peripheral vision, I hear Nessa scream Jack's name. Simon looms over him with a lunatic grin, hand fisted on the knife handle, the blade with my blood still on it glimmering and I'm thinking, *my God, he's gonna do it, he's gonna kill Jack.* There's a brick on the ground. I snatch it up without thinking, lift my arms, and crack it on the back of Simon's skull. He turns to me, eyes wide, shocked surprise, aiming his knife at my face. So I hit him again, brick against forehead. His mouth moves like a beached trout, but there are no words. Blood comes oozing through his hair. He growls in the back of his throat and falls forward.

Jack and I take two steps back and stare at the fallen body of Simon, both of us struggling to catch our breaths.

"Is he dead?" Jack's entire face is white, even his lips.

Dead. The word echoes in some chamber of my brain and my whole body seizes up like I'm paralyzed.

"I don't know," I say in a whisper, unable to take my eyes off Simon's motionless body. "I just wanted him to leave us alone."

Nessa stands with us, staring down in horror at Simon. As we watch, his right hand twitches and he takes a deep, shuddering breath, like his soul had started slithering away then decided to return to his pathetic body after all. He moans. I didn't kill him. Thank God. I messed him up bad, but I did not kill him.

"We need to bolt, Nessa," Jack says, still not taking his eyes off Simon. "Get our stuff. We'll find a new place."

Nessa nods and ducks into the shack. She comes back out with a stuffed backpack slung over her skinny shoulders. The last thing she grabs is the colored plastic bead necklace decorating the front of the shack.

"Hank," she says then in a quivery voice. "You're bleeding."

A circle of red darkens the side of my sweatshirt. I lift it up and look at my stomach, to the right of my belly button, below my ribs. A trickle of blood slides down my side and into the waistband of my pants.

"He just nicked me. I'm okay," I tell her, but everything is getting blurry around the edges. *Blood. So much blood.*

From somewhere up above there's a clanking sound and the muffled voices of men shouting to each other.

"The construction guys are showing up for work," Jack says in a panic. "Let's get out of here." But first he kneels down and reaches shaking fingers into Simon's pockets. Simon groans, but doesn't struggle. Jack pulls out a thin wallet and opens it to see a small wad of cash and a couple cards. He stuffs the wallet into his back pocket.

"Hey, what are you kids doing down there?"

Jack, Nessa, and I freeze. A man in a yellow hard hat leans out of a second floor window. I imagine the scene he sees below: Simon crumpled on the ground by the Dumpster, head oozing blood, Jack rifling through his pockets while Nessa and I stand there and watch. Accomplices. Immediately the three of us scatter, almost tripping over our feet to escape that reeking alley and the dark nameless thing that happened here.

The worker shouts something else, but we don't stop running until we've hit one of the main avenues where morning people crowd the sidewalk, hoping we can blend in. We make ourselves slow down, calm down, walk in rhythm with the stream of anonymous, innocent city people.

"Where we going, Jack?" I ask, pushing back the panic rising in my throat. There's a spatter of blood on Jack's ear, more on the front of his T-shirt. Simon's blood. I press my right arm hard against my side to hide the growing circle of my own blood, so dizzy I can't see straight.

"Somewhere safe," Jack says through clenched teeth. "Don't pass out on me now, Hank. We're almost there."

People, buildings, dogs, telephone poles, mailboxes pass in a blur, colors and blending shapes. I concentrate on moving one foot, then the other. Just keep moving. Jack and Nessa lead me to a side street, then down a set of stairs leading to a below-street-level apartment. My knees almost buckle as I scramble down the stairs behind them. I scan the street for anyone who might be chasing us, as Jack pounds on a graffiti-covered black door.

"Magpie, let me in," he shouts at the door. "It's Jack."

The sound of sirens rises from a short distance away, getting louder. Jack pounds harder on the door. "Magpie, we're in trouble. You gotta let us in."

Slowly the black door opens, and the three of us fall inside. The lights are dim in the apartment, which smells of rancid garbage, cigarette smoke, and aftershave. The weird combination of smells makes me gag. The apartment is a mess, piled nearly to the ceiling with stacks of books and newspapers and trash.

Sirens grow louder until they pass in front of the apartment. We stand motionless and silent as the wailing sound fades.

"This better be good," says the tall man standing beside the door. He has an English accent and is wearing a blue satin robe. With his beak nose and slicked black hair, Magpie resembles his name. "Talk to me."

So Jack tells Magpie everything. By the time he gets to the part about Simon and the brick, and the construction worker seeing us, my legs won't hold me up for one more second. I slump to the floor, remembering the blood, remembering the bitterness mixed with powdered sugar on my tongue. A black, heavy wave sweeps up behind my eyes.

Just before the wave crashes over my head, I hear Magpie curse at Jack, followed by a sickening smack and a cry of pain. Then I am gone.

4

THE CABIN IS TUCKED UNDER THE PINE TREES, JUST UP THE
embankment from the lake. It's small, just one room, no
bigger than a walk-in closet with windows and a fireplace. But everything is right where I need it. Just enough
space and no more. There's a narrow bed with a rough
wool blanket. A small green table and work desk. Three
chairs. A fireplace for warmth and cooking.

A large bird with a sleek black head and long blue tail
feathers is perched outside on the windowsill. He pecks
against the glass, like he wants to get in. I lie still on the
bed, try to ignore him. Inside the cabin with doors and
windows shut tight, I believe I am safe.

But the bird pecks harder, faster, like a jackhammer
against the glass, his head a black blur. Finally, the

window can't hold up. It cracks, jagged fault lines pointing fingers of lightning. Then the window breaks into a million pieces, shatters in on the bed, on me, and the big black bird swoops into the cabin, wingspan so large it fills the room, and he comes at my face.

Flailing, I fight off the bird, push his black wings away, throw fists at his sleek black head.

"Young man, stop. I'm trying to help you." Man's voice, English accent.

My eyes fly open, and there is the guy with the beak nose, holding my arms down on the floor, his black beady eyes shining with irritation. Behind him are Jack and Nessa, white-faced, concern creasing their foreheads. Jack's eye looks red and swollen and there's a fresh bruise on his cheek. I sit up too quickly and my heartbeat swishes loud in my ears.

"Tell me, do you always faint at the sight of blood?" Magpie asks. "Clearly, you have quite the delicate constitution." He rises to his feet, throwing a red-stained dishtowel over one shoulder. "You have a wound, but you were very lucky. It's not too deep. We stopped the bleeding and patched you up."

Lifting up my torn sweatshirt, I see a square of gauze taped onto my skin with a stain of blood in the center. "Thank you," I murmur.

Jack and Nessa help me stand. "What happened to your face?" I ask Jack. He glances at Magpie, at his straight back as he walks past a chaos of cardboard boxes and plastic bags into an adjoining room. Jack shakes his head at me. Nessa just looks terrified.

"Come into the kitchen," Magpie says. "I'll make breakfast and we can have ourselves a nice little chat."

Unlike the rest of his disgusting apartment, Magpie's kitchen is as neat and tidy as he is, or at least as he appears to be. Countertops are clean, silver appliances glimmer. There's actually a vase of white flowers on the table. Somehow, this guy is a neat freak and a total hoarding slob at the same time.

He makes us pancakes and sausage links, and even though I don't have any appetite at all, I take a few bites so I won't insult him. While we try to eat the food he cooked, Magpie calmly discusses our future options with us.

"In short, you are completely screwed," he says, sounding ridiculously formal with his British accent. "So what are we to do with you? The cops will likely be searching for the three of you together, so the first thing you need to do is split up." He dunks a tea bag into a flowered teacup. "Jack, go to Port Authority and look up Ginger and Watchdog. They'll know what to do with you." Jack slumps slightly but doesn't say a word. "Miss Vanessa, I've called my connections uptown and they're prepared to give you a makeover within the hour. I think blond hair would suit you." Nessa pokes at a sausage with her fork.

Magpie's glance reaches me, and his eyes sweep me from head to toe, as if I'm some racehorse he might consider buying. "Thank you, Jack, for bringing Henry to me, although obviously, I would've preferred less dire circumstances."

What does he mean by "bringing" me to him? I slide narrowed eyes at Jack, but he won't look at me.

"Now, what shall we do with you, Henry?" Magpie taps a shiny fingernail against his china teacup.

I glance at Jack's bruised face and the black eye that's turning purple, then at Magpie. His fancy robe gaps open at the chest and I glimpse what looks like a grayish T-shirt underneath. I bet he sits around in his dirty underwear all day and only covers himself with that classy-looking robe when someone comes to the door.

Not waiting for me to respond, Magpie blows on his steaming cup of tea and takes a sip. "I believe it's fair to say you work for me now." He sets his cup back down on the polished wood table. "Understand?"

Magpie sits all formal and proper at his table, but I sense sharp talons, a razor-sharp beak, black wings beating at my face. I know I should pretend to agree with him, but instead I shake my head and whisper, "No."

Out of the corner of my eye I see the desperate, warning glances I'm getting from Jack and Nessa, but I ignore them.

Magpie smiles and tilts his head to the side, like maybe he's really fond of me. He stands and gets something out of a drawer next to the sink. There's a flash of metal and before I can react, the barrel of a gun jams into my cheek so hard I swear it almost knocks out a molar. There's a loud click as Magpie cocks back the hammer.

"Maybe you woke up yesterday morning on your own, but things are different now. You know the kind of business I do, or at least you have an idea. You assaulted one of my clients in that alley. And now you know where I live. We are in this together, Henry. Do we understand each other?" Cold metal invades my face. Slowly, I nod.

Magpie grins at me and removes the gun from my cheek. "Good boy. Welcome to the family." He smacks me on the back like a kind uncle. "Now first off, you need to bathe and put on some different clothes. I think you'd clean up quite nicely, given half a chance." He looks me up and down. "Yes, indeed. You'll do just fine." He turns toward the sink and places the gun back in its drawer. "Vanessa, darling, do the dishes, won't you? Jack, get Henry cleaned up. I think you'll find something just about his size in the bedroom closet."

❧

Without a word, Jack leads me into another room, presumably Magpie's bedroom. Except for a fancy four-poster bed in the corner covered with a shiny smoothed-down purple bedspread, every surface of the room is buried in more junk. There is broken furniture and piles of old clothes, cardboard boxes overflowing with empty wine bottles and fast food wrappers. And strangest of all, clusters of moldy-looking teddy bears and a broken baby crib.

Magpie is as much a neat freak in his bathroom as his kitchen, and when I step into a sparkling shower stall, I have my choice of shampoos, conditioners, and scented soaps. I choose the least girly-smelling products, and wince as they come into contact with the cut on my side. I pull off the soaked bandage, and it doesn't look good. It's deeper than Magpie led me to believe and it's starting to bleed again. After I get out of the shower, I see a fresh bandage laid out on top of a dry towel. Magpie— or at least the neat-freak organized part of him—thought of everything. I dry off, put the new bandage on my cut, and tuck the towel around my waist.

Even if I'm forced for the moment to play nice with Magpie and his gun, I know one thing for sure: as soon as I get the hell out of this apartment, I will run and run and never look back.

Jack leads me into an enormous walk-in closet attached to the bathroom. On one side of the room are men's clothes and shoes. Pressed dress shirts are lined up by color. On the other side of the room are shelves with neatly folded pants and sweaters. A freestanding full-length mirror fills one corner. I wonder when Magpie last wore any of these clothes or wore anything besides old underwear and his fancy blue robe.

"Here, Hank. I think this is what Magpie was thinking." He pulls out a pair of jeans, folded neatly over a hanger. Then he chooses a white collared shirt and a green sweater and hands them both to me. Without making eye contact, he disappears and I hear the shower running.

I put on the clothes, which are a little loose but fit okay, then I brush the last of the dried mud off my sneakers into a wastebasket and put them back on.

Standing in front of the mirror, I take in my new look. And to be honest, I look nice. Kinda preppy for my taste, but it'll do.

"I knew you'd shine up like a brand new penny."

I swing around, and see Magpie standing at the door of the closet, smiling at me, friendly and creepy at the same time.

"I'll probably have to burn these other clothes of yours, but you won't be needing them anymore." He holds up a plastic trash bag. When he brought in the bandage, he must have grabbed my clothes from where I'd left them on the floor. Along with my book.

Panic prickles my scalp. "My book—"

Magpie smiles again. "Ah, a youngster after my own heart, a true lover of fine literature. I would never get between a man and his copy of *Walden*."

He reaches into the bag and holds out my book. I snatch it out of his hand. "Uh. Thank you," I say to soften my rudeness.

Magpie cocks his head to the side and chuckles. "I, too, am an avid student of the transcendentalists," he announces, loving the sound of his own voice. "Thoreau, Emerson, Whitman. Certainly they are the best of your American writers."

Whatever. Being alone with this guy makes me want

to take another hot shower and scrub my skin raw. I'm relieved when Jack finishes his shower and joins us.

After Jack, Nessa, and I are clean and dressed, Magpie lines us up and takes a good look at us.

"All right," he says. "You know what to do now." He smiles, and for a moment I think he's genuinely pleased with all of us. But then his face turns cold and stiff as a mask. "Now the three of you get the hell out of my house. And don't be so careless again, you stupid little shits."

He waves a hand at us. Dismissed.

Out on the street, Nessa presses her forehead against Jack's before they say good-bye. He whispers something to her, and she nods. Her eyes are full of tears. Then she comes over to me. Those big eyes without makeup are so damn pretty, blue like the sky before twilight. I just want to hold her, imagine her heart beating fast against my chest.

"Thanks for saving Jack's life," she whispers in my ear. Then she goes up on tiptoe and touches her lips to mine. Not just a peck, but a soft, full-out kiss that she allows to linger. She gives my hand a hard squeeze, and then, as if I'd imagined her all along, she vanishes into the crowd.

"Wow," I say to Jack, trying to be casual. "Did you see that? Your girlfriend just planted one on me."

"She's not my girlfriend," he says in a quiet voice. "She's my sister."

Sister. My heart stops beating, and I forget to breathe.

"Hank? You okay?"

"Yeah. Sorry."

Sister. The word stirs something inside me. So far, it's just a word, but I sense it's the beginning of a solid memory, and it doesn't have skin on yet. The beast twitches inside me, and I feel sick. Push the thought away for now.

"So Nessa and your dad…"

"Yeah, he was hurting her too." He swallows hard and his Adam's apple bobs in his throat. "This life sucks, but it's still better than being home. With him."

"So you'd rather get smacked around by Magpie than your own dad?" Man. I feel bad as soon as I say it.

He glares at me, his black eye gleaming like an accusation. "Shut up, Hank."

"Jack, I'm sorry. But I don't get why you're going to do everything Magpie tells you. The guy is a psychopath."

"I have no choice till this thing blows over, Hank. And neither do you. He'll protect us. But at the same time, he's got us by the balls."

"Only if we let him." I shake my head at him as betrayal and wounded righteousness wash over me. "And just because you delivered me to Magpie as some pathetic new recruit, doesn't mean I have to cooperate."

At least Jack has the decency to look ashamed. "You don't know anything, Hank," he murmurs.

We stand on a street corner and after the light changes, Jack tries to lead us to the right, but I go left, back toward Penn Station.

"Hank, it's this way. We gotta go to Port Authority to meet up with Ginger and Watchdog."

I keep walking, in the opposite direction of Magpie and his directives. As far away as possible. "Who are they, anyway?"

"They work with Magpie," Jack says, trotting to keep up with me. "They're expecting us, and believe me, the last thing you want to do is piss them off."

I grip my copy of *Walden* tight in my hand and keep walking.

The cabin in my dream was just like the one that Thoreau built. I know as I stare at the cover of the book, at the trees and the pond, *that's where I want to be*, that I will not spend another night in the city. I will not look at the moon through smog, will not breathe taxicab exhaust, or listen to the beeps of a hundred car horns. And in spite of my dream, if I can make it to the cabin, I believe the black bird will never find me.

I'm walking faster and faster, till I'm running down the street, dodging men and women in suits going to work, parents holding little kids' hands on their way to school. Normal people starting a normal day. People who didn't just get attacked in an alley and crack some guy in the head with a brick. Maybe I can outrun all of it.

"Come on, Hank," Jack shouts after me, but I refuse to slow down. He pleads with me the whole way to Penn Station, to the entrance, down the escalator, into the terminal. Even though the cut in my side throbs with every footfall, it feels so good to run. Escaping. Like I'm running away from something horrible and running to something better. Something different anyway, and different is good.

Finally in the lobby of the train station, Jack grabs my arm and makes me look into his face. "Were you some track star in your former life? Goddamn." He's breathing hard and his cheeks are bright red. "Hank, listen to me. You're in this now. If you run, they're going to chase you, and if they find you, there's a good chance they'll kill you. They might hurt me too for letting you get away."

"Then why would you stay here?" I glance up at the train schedule board over his head, suspended from the ceiling in the center of the terminal. "Get on a train and get the hell out of here."

"I can't, Hank. This sucks, but at least we know how to survive here. We know our way around, you know? Doesn't sound like much, but it's all we've got."

So even if your life is crap, you'll hold on to it just because it's familiar? I almost say this out loud to Jack, but I stop myself. Beacause in truth, I get it. Absolutely nothing in my life is familiar, and it's like standing on the edge of a cliff every damn minute, rocks crumbling under my feet.

A guarded, suspicious look crosses Jack's face like a shadow. "I thought you said you didn't have any money, Hank."

"I don't."

"Then you're a fucking liar. How are you going to buy yourself a train ticket if you don't have money?"

My heart sinks. What am I thinking? Exhausted, I sink down on the floor of the terminal against the wall, and crack my head against the tile as self-punishment. It makes the lump on my head throb but I don't even care.

"You think just because you're wearing a nice outfit and look like a J.Crew model, they're going to just give you a seat for free?" Jack shakes his head, like he actually feels sorry for me. "You must be used to your nice, rich daddy paying for everything so you don't even have to think about it."

Wow. Is that it? Do I have a rich father who buys me things so that in real life I take money for granted? I try to create an image of this wealthy, generous father, but nothing comes.

"Maybe," is all I can manage around the lump in my throat. "I don't remember."

Jack sits down on the floor next to me and stares into my face for a long time. "Look," he finally says. "Nessa and me, we can't go home. But maybe where you're from is worth going back to." He reaches into his back pocket and takes out a brown leather wallet. Simon's wallet. "Take this."

My mind's eye flashes to blood, Simon's body twitching in the alley. You'd think the thing was on fire the way I jerked my hand away.

"Take it," Jack says, fiercer this time. "You saved my life. Plus, there's this other thing." He bites his cheek and stares over my shoulder, like there's something really interesting there. "You were right. I recruited you, or whatever. Brought you to Magpie on purpose. And he gave me money for it."

I stare at him.

"What, like a bonus or something?"

"Yeah, exactly like that." Jack won't meet my eyes. "So, come on, take it."

My fingers tingle at the touch of the soft, worn leather, but I accept the wallet. It's old and cracked, and there are initials on the front, SJG. Simon must have been a real person before he was a junkie. Someone with initials, who was proud enough to have them engraved on his wallet. I peek inside. There's a paper social security card with the name Simon James Grady. A library card from Dubuque, Iowa. And money. At least two hundred dollars.

"Hey." There's a gruff voice beside us and I smell unwashed body, a familiar odor like onion soup gone bad. "You gonna eat that?"

Jack rolls his eyes. "Frankie, get the hell away from us."

Frankie's bloodshot eyes are lasered in on the wallet.

"Dammit," Jack says.

We try to move to a different corner of the terminal, but Frankie lumbers after us. We ignore him. We don't have much time.

"Jack, you need to leave too. Seriously. Go find Nessa, and get away from here."

Jack shakes his head and nervously scans the terminal.

"Don't worry about us. I'll think of something to tell Magpie. You didn't get to see it, but I think he really likes us. He says we're more special to him than any of the other kids, and I believe him. We'll be okay, I promise."

I bite my lip, and my eyeballs sting. I don't want to leave Jack and Nessa behind in this place. But I can't stay either.

Jack rubs his nose with the heel of his hand. "So where you going, Hank?"

I clutch the book. "*I'm going to go to the woods to live deliberately*," I say. "*To front only the essential facts of life, and see if I can learn what it has to teach, and not, when I come to die, discover that I had not lived.*"

"You're going to *what*?"

I pause. The words are Thoreau's, from the book. I saw them like a photograph in my brain and just blurted them out. "Never mind," I say to Jack.

"You. Gonna. Eat. That?"

We look up in exasperation at Frankie, who is still hovering near us. He won't stop staring at my back pocket, where I stuffed the wallet. "Frankie, stop staring at my ass," I say. He ignores me and keeps his eyes locked.

Jack peers over Frankie's shoulder and freezes. "Shit," he says. I turn and see two transit cops on the other side of the terminal, a heavyset, dark-haired woman, and a burly guy who takes off his police cap to scratch his head, revealing a military-style blond buzz cut. They stop a kid about our age with dark hair like mine and ask him a lot of questions.

"I gotta go," Jack says, not taking his eyes off the cops. "Be safe, Hank."

"Take care of yourself, Jack. And Nessa."

He gives me a crooked smile. "I always do." He turns and latches on to a family with two little girls who are walking by. "Excuse me," I hear him say. "But do you know when the train to Washington DC leaves?"

Certainly the cops will assume this is his family and not be suspicious, the way he's talking so easy with them, laughing and joking. Damn, he's good. But aside from Frankie, who doesn't count, I'm a kid all alone. And if the word is out about the assault in the alley this morning, they'll be on the lookout for three kids. One of them who looks exactly like me.

The cops have stopped questioning the kid and are heading in my direction. Luckily they haven't spotted me yet, which is good, since I'm gawking at them in full-out panic mode. After all, I now have Simon's wallet on me, evidence to connect me very solidly with a crime. It has his initials for chrissakes. And his ID. I am so screwed. Quickly, I take out all the cash and stuff it into my front pocket, ready to ditch the wallet. Frankie watches every move with his beady eyes, but I'm too terrified to deal with him.

As I watch them, the woman cop looks in my direction, then gives me a double-take. She looks tough, like she'd really enjoy being the one to nail my ass to the wall. I glance away quickly, but she and her buzz-cut partner are heading straight for me. I won't have a chance to dump the wallet in the trash without them being suspicious.

"You…gonna…"

I stare blankly at Frankie and pull the wallet out of my back pocket. He licks his lips and looks expectant. As casually as possible, with my back to the cops, I hand Frankie the social security card. He grins, takes it from me with a pinky extended, and pops the whole thing in his mouth. In one chew and swallow, it is gone. I hand him the library card, and it, too, vanishes. Digesting the evidence. So far, so good. Bless you, Frankie, bless you.

Turning back toward the transit cops, I see they're almost on me. But then this lady in a purple knit hat darts in front of them, eyes up on the destination screen, and she smacks right into the burly cop. In the confusion, I grip the wallet, hoping for the impossible. Paper is one thing, but can Frankie actually eat a wallet? "You gonna…" I drop it on the floor, and kick it to the tips of his dusty black boots.

"Take it!"

And so he does. He reaches down, licking his chops like the wallet is a juicy porterhouse steak, and takes a huge bite out of it. Fortunately, the wallet is old, and this dude has strong teeth. He literally rips a piece of leather right out of the wallet, chews once, and swallows. Then he's back for another. Bite, chew, swallow. The cops are almost on us now, and I can still see Simon's initials on the side, SJG. Faster, I think. You can do it, Frankie. Bite, chew, swallow.

Before they can speak, I turn to the cops like I've just noticed them and manage an expression of total outrage. "Officers, do you see what this man is doing?" I sputter. "I dropped my wallet on the ground—he picked it up, and now"—I gesture helplessly, and the three of us look at Frankie—"he's eating it."

Frankie glances at each of us and grins, still chewing on leather and drooling into his beard. The front of the wallet, the part with the initials, is almost gone, except for the first letter, *S*.

"Frankie, did you take this boy's wallet?" The woman asks in an annoyed tone. Frankie shakes his massive head and swallows. "Mine."

"What's your name, son?" Buzz Cut asks me.

I almost say *Henry. Henry David.* But we are all looking down at the wallet and the remaining initial. "Steven," I say quickly. "Steven David. Son. Davidson." Awkward, but I think I pulled it off.

"Give the boy his wallet," Buzz Cut says to Frankie. Apparently Frankie has respect for authority, because he hands it over, the same way he'd relinquished the book yesterday.

The cop looks over my shoulder when I open the soggy wallet to peer inside. "Looks like he cleaned you out. Come on, Frankie, you need to give this boy his money back."

"No, it's okay, he didn't take my money." I say. "I, uh, before I came into the city, my parents told me I should always keep my money in a front pocket." Stupidly, I pat my front pocket to illustrate. "They said there are a lot of bad people in the city, so you have to be careful." My palms are sweaty and I try not to think about Simon, afraid they'll be able to magically read my mind. "So I'm okay for now, officers. Thank you for your assistance." That last part might have been slightly over the top.

The lady cop looks me over, and I hold my breath.

"So where are you headed, Steven?"

"Home," I say.

"And where's that?"

I conjure a picture in my head of the destination board and spout off the first city on the sign. "Philadelphia."

"Ahh, nice town. Eagles fan?"

"Yes, ma'am."

Her friendly manner vanishes, and she puts a hand on her hip, next to her gun.

"I need to see an ID please, Steven," she says.

"Of course," I say. Sweat is dripping down the back of my neck. I open the wallet again, pretend to search all the sections that might hold an ID. "It's not here," I say, going for a look of distress.

We all turn eyes on Frankie.

"Did you eat this boy's ID, Frankie?" Buzz Cut asks.

Frankie grins and smiles, a little spit shimmering on his bottom lip.

Lady Cop looks me over, taking in my polite smile and my clean, supremely preppy ensemble. If the construction worker's description is out, she'll be looking for a dark-haired kid in a grimy blood-covered sweatshirt and torn jeans. Even so, I hold my breath until she says, "I'm sorry you had a run-in with Frankie here. When you get home, make sure you make some calls to replace your ID and anything else Frankie here might have ingested."

"I will," I promise.

"Okay, kid. Hope the rest of your day goes better." Buzz Cut gives me a fatherly pat on the arm. "Have a good trip home, Steven."

I buy my ticket and as soon as they announce the all-aboard for my trip, I double-time it down the escalator, push past slower people lined up to board the train, and immediately find a seat.

Up until the second the train pulls out of the station, I'm sure someone—Magpie with his gun or a cop with handcuffs—is going to come for me. But miraculously, no one does. No one seems to notice me at all.

5

Twenty minutes into the four-hour ride to Boston, I finally relax, going over my itinerary in my head over and over again to settle my twitchy brain. The train will arrive at South Station in Boston. The lady in the ticket booth told me I should take a cab to North Station. And from there, a commuter train to Concord. If all goes well, I should get in about 4 p.m. today.

As for what happens after that, I have no idea. I'm trying not to think about that part. For now, I'm safe and warm, and sitting in this really comfortable chair watching the scenery go by. Buildings and bridges and concrete switch over to houses and trees and rivers. A lot of the tall grass I see is still kind of brown, and the trees just have buds on them, so I figure it's early spring sometime. A glance at the date stamped on my train ticket confirms it. Mid-April.

From the dining car at the middle of the train, I buy two hot dogs and take my time eating them. On the outside, I must look completely normal to people around me, who barely give me a second look. Just some kid eating hot dogs on the train to Boston.

But as soon as I'm alone with my thoughts, total panic is a heartbeat away. Is this really happening? Did I really almost kill a guy in an alley? What the hell kind of person am I? Simon's face, shocked and bloody, swims into my consciousness and it's a struggle to keep the hot dogs down. There is nothing "normal" about me. I have a knife injury that I have to press paper towels against to control the bleeding. I assaulted a guy in an alley. I came close to becoming Magpie's property in his creepy, surreal world of street kids and drugs. I'm worried about Jack and Nessa, who are still out on the streets, in danger. And then of course, there's that other detail—I still have no idea who I am.

Can't stand it. Have to think of something else or I'm going to curl up into a ball with my hands over my ears and start screaming.

Walden. I open the book with shaky hands and start to read, will myself to get lost in this book that might hold some clues for me. Completely submerge myself in the world I'm on my way to see.

I'm a crazy fast reader and finish most of the book even before we reach Massachusetts. Of course, there are pages missing here and there because of Frankie, but I can use my imagination to fill in the blanks.

To sum up—if I've got it right—this Thoreau guy was tired of civilization and how people become slaves to their own stupid houses and possessions. To prove he could be happier without those things, he stripped his life down to the simplest things he knew and took off to live alone in the woods. It sounds like he was really happy and at peace when he was in the woods like that, living by a pond. Must have been nice.

The lull of the train, swaying and click-clacking down the track makes me sleepy. I close my eyes.

My house was on the side of a hill, immediately on the edge of the larger wood, in the midst of a young forest of pitch pines and hickories, and half a dozen rods from the pond, to which a narrow footpath led down the hill.

The words appear like they've been etched on the inside of my eyelids. I recognize them as words I just read in *Walden*, but what the hell? Startled, I shake the words out of my head and stare out the window at the scenery, trying to clear my mind, just sleep. My eyes drift shut again.

I find it wholesome to be alone the greater part of the

time. To be in company, even with the best, is soon weari-
some and dissipating. I love to be alone. I never found the
companion that was so companionable as solitude.

It happens again. Whenever I close my eyes, entire
pages and paragraphs of the book appear in my brain
like snapshots in an album. If I wanted to, I could recite
whole passages of *Walden* to the people sitting around
me. I really could.

If a man does not keep pace with his companions, perhaps
it is because he hears a different drummer. Let him step to
the music which he hears, however measured or far away.

Okay, so this is getting annoying. Maybe because
I have so little information stored in my stupid brain,
I can retain entire pages of the first book I remember
reading. I guess that makes sense. Sort of.

I learned this, at least, by my experiment; that if one
advances confidently in the direction of his dreams, and
endeavors to live the life which he has imagined, he will meet
with a success unexpected in common hours.

After playing around with this bizarre phenomenon
for a while, it occurs to me that what I've got has a name:
photographic memory. And I almost laugh out loud,
right there in the train. I'm a kid with amnesia and a
photographic memory. Can't remember anything that
happened to me before around midnight last night, but

everything I've read since then is chiseled into my brain. Talk about a memory gone completely twisted.

❦

"Concord, CON-cord!" bellows the train conductor as he whips my ticket stub from a clip on the seat in front of me. Pressing my face to the smudged window, I watch the town of Concord come into view, then wipe away my fog breath with my sleeve.

It's possible that as soon as I step off the train in Concord, my whole life will come back to me in a rush. Or that somebody will recognize me and take me home. Would that be good or bad? Would I be taken to a house and family where I'm safe and loved, or will the police nab me on the streets of Concord? I have absolutely no idea. But I have to start somewhere. And this is it.

The train jolts to a stop, and I line up behind the other people getting ready to step off the train and onto the platform. The late-afternoon sun slants orange through a big maple tree when I step off the train, nearly blinding me, so my first view of Concord is splotched with stars. I blink hard to get rid of them, then take a few steps off the train platform and just stand there in a small parking lot, making the other people walk around me, some peering back at me in curiosity. I watch everybody. Do they know me? Will they call me by the name I can't remember? Is this home? Nobody shows any recognition. I'm both relieved and disappointed.

Across from the depot is a restaurant with clumps of yellow flowers planted out front and next to that is a bicycle shop and a dry cleaner's. There are trees and shrubs on both sides of the narrow street, and everything looks scrubbed and clean, like maybe somebody comes out and washes the sidewalks every morning. A cool breeze blows my hair into my eyes.

Even as I absorb Concord, Massachusetts, even as I scan the street, searching people's faces, one thing is clear to me: I have no memory of this place. It's just a nice little town where people probably feel safe all the time and have nice families to go home to. A town where you don't have to worry about junkies in alleys pulling knives on you. I wonder if Concord even has alleys.

The train bell clangs behind me, and the train pulls away from the platform. All the other people are gone. I bite my lip so hard it hurts.

There's nothing else to do, so I step onto the sidewalk, look both ways and randomly head to the right. There's a gas station at the corner, a doughnut shop across the street. When I reach the curb, I squint up at the street sign. Sudbury Road is the crossroad heading off to the right. I twist my head to get a good look at the name of the other road, the one I'm currently standing on.

Thoreau Street. The name of the place on which I stand is Thoreau Street. I stare down in amazement at Thoreau's book in my hands, as if it somehow magically made this phenomenon happen and can tell me what I'm supposed to do next.

When I glance up again, there's a girl standing next to me, waiting for the light to change so she can cross the street. She's pretty in a girl-jock kind of way, with reddish blond hair in a ponytail, navy blue shorts, and a yellow T-shirt that says Concord Lacrosse. I search her face, hoping to see something familiar there. *Do I know you? Do you know me?* It's not until she turns to gaze directly back at me that I realize how rudely I've been staring.

"Uh, hi," I say, trying—too late—to be polite. Then, I cut my eyes away and stare down at the sidewalk. But still, I feel her eyes on me, checking me out pretty much the same way I'd been doing to her. I wait for the light to change so I can escape.

"Hi back," she says after a moment. "You look…"

I tense up, expecting her to say something like, "you look like that criminal I saw on TV last night," or "you look like somebody who lives in this town and vanished mysteriously a few weeks ago."

"…lost," she says. Her face is open, so different from the cautious eyes and shifty glances of people in the city. I guess when people are safe, they can afford to be friendly.

"I am lost." My mouth is dry and my voice comes out like a croak. "Could you tell me how to get—"

"To Walden Pond?"

I stare at her. "How did you know?"

She points at the book in my hand. "The book. Another friend of Thoreau. We're used to it around here."

"Oh," I mumble, oddly embarrassed to be just another random follower of Henry in this girl's eyes.

"Well, I can show you how to get there. It's not far, less than a mile. I came into town for Starbucks, but now I'm headed back to the high school for the late bus. If you walk with me, that'll get you most of the way there."

She looks sideways at me, and her ponytail swings behind her. Girls. Do I know anything about them? How to act with them, what they want? All I can say for sure is that I already like this girl, ans so far she seems to like me back.

"All right," I say. "Which way?"

She points in the direction I'm already heading on

Thoreau Street. "Walden Pond is just past the high school, across the highway."

Walden Pond is within walking distance. Good. After all that sitting, I'd much rather walk than take a cab. If they even have cabs in Concord, Massachusetts. It seems like the kind of place where they automatically award every kid a Mercedes as soon as he or she passes driver's ed.

"I'm Hailey, by the way," she says as we approach the first crosswalk. She pauses, looks up at me expectantly.

The name thing again. I almost blurt out "Henry David," with more conviction than that first time with Jack, but catch myself just in time. Here I am, holding a copy of *Walden*, on my way to Walden Pond on Thoreau Street in Concord. No doubt about it, that's going to sound suspicious.

"I'm Hank," I say. Last names seem unimportant to Hailey, who nods and swishes her ponytail again.

"Where you from, Hank?"

I clear my throat, trying to buy time. "You first."

She has a pretty smile. Bright, trusting green eyes. And there's something sweet and fragile in her that reminds me of Nessa.

"Just up on Authors Ridge. You know, up near the cemetery where Emerson and Alcott are buried."

"Of course," I say, pretending to know who they are. Emerson is one of the writers Magpie mentioned when we were in his closet, but the name is all I know.

We pass a line of Victorian houses painted white and yellow and green, all with big front porches and shutters. After the claustrophobic vibe of the city, the town feels open, with wide expanses of lawn and blue sky.

"And…where are you from, Hank?" Hailey prompts.

"Well, I'm from, uh, near Boston. Probably moving to Concord soon."

Hailey pulls the hairband out of her hair, tucks it between her front teeth and gathers the hair back together to bunch back into a ponytail. "Yeah?" she asks through the hairband. "When?"

"Um. I'm not really sure. I mean, my parents work in Boston and want to move out of the city. When we find a house, that is." I'm surprised by how smoothly these lies slip out.

"Do you have brothers and sisters?" Hailey asks me.

I get ready to say *one of each*, the first response that comes to me, but that's not what comes out of my mouth. "Just a sister," I say.

"Are you okay, Hank?"

I've stopped walking and am leaning over at the waist, staring down at the concrete sidewalk. *Sister.* That word again. Like a punch in the gut. I have a flash of something, shredded edge of memory. A sense of danger, panic. Is my sister is in trouble? My gut seems to think so.

"Hank?"

"Sorry. Yeah, I'm okay." I push the memory back before the beast can claw at my insides. "It's just, um." I catch a glimpse of Hailey's T-shirt from the corner of my eye. *Concord Lacrosse.* "My leg. I pulled a hamstring running track. Sometimes it just zings me, you know?" I rub the back of my leg for dramatic effect, wondering about the lie that wouldn't come out and then the one that came so easy.

Hailey nods. "My cousin did that once, pulled a hamstring playing basketball. Sucks." This jock-girl knows her sports injuries. "You gonna make it, Hank?"

"Yep. I think I'll survive." I limp through a few steps to appear convincing.

We get to a big wooden sign that reads, HENRY DAVID THOREAU REGIONAL HIGH SCHOOL, near the entrance of a wide driveway. I almost laugh out loud. Is everything in this town named after Thoreau?

"Come on up and see the school," Hailey says. "Since you might be moving here and all." I follow her up the driveway.

Thoreau High School is small, just one story high, made of yellow concrete bricks. The bushes out front are early spring sparse, with little buds that seem a long way from opening. We pass a playing field with a scoreboard that says, *Home of the Patriots.* Kids are running around on the playing fields, practicing baseball and soccer and track. Some kids are just milling around, sitting on fences, talking and laughing. A few stare openly as we walk past them, and I feel sweat on the back of my neck.

Can they see I'm an imposter? That I have no identity and no memory? I adjust my walk to longer, more confident strides and stare back with hardened eyes, holding their glances hostage until they are forced to look away.

"Hey, Danielle," Hailey says to a tall blond girl near the entrance of the building. She's wearing a lacrosse uniform like Hailey's, although in comparison, the baggy clothes look shapeless on her.

Danielle smiles. "Hailey," she says, cutting a friendly, curious glance at me. But she looks back at Hailey and her smile falls. "Girl, you're pale. You need some juice or something?"

"I'm fine," says Hailey quickly. But I take a good look at her and see that Danielle's right. Her cheeks, which should've been flushed from walking a mile in the cold

April air, are white. I'd been too distracted by my surroundings to notice, which makes me feel like a jerk.

"I might have some candy in my backpack," Danielle says.

"I told you. I'm *fine*," Hailey says, this time through clenched teeth.

Glancing from one to the other, I don't know what to do, other than change the subject and distract everybody. I clear my throat. "Hi," I say to Danielle. "I'm Hank."

Danielle looks me over, and her smile returns.

"I found him near the train station," Hailey says. "Trying to find Walden Pond."

"Hello, Hank," Danielle says. "Wow, you have the most gorgeous gray eyes ever."

"Dan-*yell*." Hailey flashes her friend a terse "cut it out" look. I try to hide a smile.

Danielle shrugs. "Well, he does."

I peer behind the girls into the high school building and glimpse a glass case of sports trophies and a hallway lined with lockers. Where did I go to school and what did I do? Did I actually run track? Was I smart? Did I have a cute girlfriend like Hailey who I took to school dances and made out with in my mother's car? That is, if I have a mother and if she has a car. Before another surge of blackness hits, I push these thoughts away.

"It's really nice to meet both of you," I say politely. "But I should probably get going before it gets dark, you know?" Besides, Danielle is still eyeing Hailey like she wants to give her CPR or a transfusion or something. None of my business, but I can see Hailey is embarrassed, so this would be the perfect time for me to disappear.

A flash of disappointment crosses Hailey's face, but then she recovers. "Okay, so keep walking past the school, down that road," she says, pointing off to the right. "You'll hit Route Two which is a major road, and cross over. Then all you need to do is walk like another half mile. Straight shot, lots of signs. You'll see it on your right."

"Great. Thanks."

Then she looks up at me and gives me this weird, sad little smile. Like she knows me and is sad to see me leave so soon, though in my bizarre rootless state, I could be imagining this. "So, Hank, let me know when you move to Concord, okay?"

I smile back at her. "Sure."

"Oh." She reaches into the back pocket of her shorts and pulls out a cell phone. "I should get your number then. And give you mine."

I pause for a beat. "My number?"

"Yeah. That's okay, right?"

I look at her phone. Surely I have one, or had one, back when I was a normal person. "Well, I don't have a phone right now. I'm getting a new one. With a new number." Hailey looks disappointed, like she suspects I'm trying to blow her off. "So, would you write yours down for me?" I ask quickly.

Hailey perks up again and I notice a dimple in her left cheek. "Got a piece of paper?"

"No." I pause. "But I do have this." I pull the book out of the back of my jeans and open it up to the back cover. "You can write it down here."

Danielle digs into her backpack and gives Hailey a pen. In big loopy handwriting, Hailey writes her name and phone number inside the back cover of *Walden*. For good measure, she draws a little flower next to her name.

"See you around, Hank," she says.

"Later, Hailey. Bye, Danielle."

And as I stride down the high school driveway, I feel Hailey's eyes on me, along with the eyes of her friends. To tell you the truth, it's not a bad feeling at all.

When I cross Route Two, I come to a big green sign that reads: *Walden Pond State Reservation*. Almost there.

The sounds of the highway fade as I take the road into the woods. The air is cool and fresh and smells like leaves and dirt and the pine needles crunching under my feet. I continue down the road and sense the presence of the pond even before I see it—an open space off to the right, a break in the thickness of the woods. Then, there it is, a smooth gray surface like chrome reflecting the sky.

This is exactly what I imagined last night—was it only last night?—reading behind the Dumpster, with Jack and Nessa sleeping nearby. I can't believe I'm here.

A steep walkway leads down to the water and a small sandy beach. I stand there for a while, listening to the quiet and breathing in the peacefulness of this place. A man and woman sit on a stone wall by the water, looking out at the spreading purple of the sky. A gray-haired man in hiking boots comes out of the woods and gives me a nod. Night is coming.

To Site of Thoreau's Hut

A sign with an arrow pointing to the right of the beach leads to a path along the shore of Walden Pond. The sun sinks and the temperature drops as I walk about halfway around the pond, looking for signs of the cabin.

I'm about to say screw it and just sit down for a while,

when I see another sign with the words *House Site* pointing up a small hill away from shore. Finally. I climb the hill, looking for the cabin. Instead I see a big clearing with more signs and a big pile of rocks and pebbles. But where's the cabin?

A few steps farther, and there's a group of carved stone pylons, like skinny headstones. About twelve of these waist-high stone pillars are arranged in a perfect square, and all but the two in front are attached to each other with chains. It's like some crazy outdoor exhibit at a museum. I lean over and squint in the dying light to read the words engraved on a metal sign: SITE OF THOREAU'S CABIN. DISCOVERED NOVEMBER 11, 1945.

Blinking hard, I read it again. *Site of* Thoreau's cabin. And finally, I get it. Yes, the cabin was here in this spot, a long time ago. But not anymore. Of course not anymore. I should have realized this. Stupid, stupid, stupid.

I step inside the stones outlining where the cabin used to be. It's smaller than I expected. At the back there's a flat stone with some poem about Thoreau's hearth. That spot is where his fireplace was.

The sun disappears behind the horizon and I start to shiver. I wish that cabin was still here, with a big fire in the fireplace. Maybe hot stew or something cooking in a pot. But there's nothing for me to do but gather a pile of dead leaves to make a pathetic pillow on the stone where Thoreau's hearth used to be. Lying down, I try to imagine there is still warmth in that old stone after all these years. I try to pretend there's a cabin built up around me, just like the one in my dream. I try to sleep.

❧

Well.

No matter how amazing he was, or how much he loved the whole nature thing, even Henry David Thoreau would have hated being me at Walden Pond on a night like this.

It's cold and dark, there are weird rustling noises in the woods, and I'm so lonely I feel like the last person left on earth. I'm shivering so hard my teeth rattle in my head and I would give just about anything, including my left nut, for a blanket. This sucks. At least the train station in New York was warm. I hate Thoreau for luring me here and making me think that by coming here, I might actually figure out who I am. Dozing off and waking up, suffering through surreal dreams of being chased and eaten by coyotes and rabid foxes, somehow I survive the night.

Just before dawn, the woods grow dead quiet and there's something electric in the air. Somebody—or something—is here, watching me. A presence. My eyes fly open in a panic, and I see him. Henry David Thoreau. He looks exactly like the picture on the back cover of *Walden*, his hair dark and curly, one hand gripping the lapel of an old-fashioned gray overcoat. Standing at the side of the stone pillars, he looks down and watches me shiver.

"What are you doing, boy?"

Did he really just speak or did I imagine it?

"I'm, uh, you know." My mouth is so dry I can hardly talk. "Trying to simplify, like you wrote about. Live in nature." Jesus. I sound like an idiot. But it's a little nerve-wracking to talk to a ghost. Or the dream of a ghost. Or whatever this is.

Thoreau squints down at me doubtfully. "You read my book?"

"Yes," I tell him. "Every word." Well, every word except the ones on the pages Frankie ate, but I don't want to get into that.

He smiles at me, and nods his head toward the sign by the rock pile. Thoreau's smile turns into a dry, raspy chuckle. The sound gets louder, then suddenly he's bent over at the waist, hands on his knees, laughing his ass off. At me.

What's so damn funny? I look over at the sign, at the

quote printed there in the dim morning light, even though I remember perfectly what it says:

I went to the woods because I wished to live deliberately, to front only the essential facts of life, and see if I could not learn what it had to teach, and not, when I came to die, discover that I had not lived.

No wonder Thoreau is laughing at me. There's such a thing as simplifying too much. Leave out the "essential facts of life" like food, warm clothes, and shelter, and obviously you won't be able to keep your stupid self alive.

I turn back to where Thoreau stood to say, point taken. But I don't have to cut back on too much stuff or food or money or a big house. I'm here, starting from absolutely nowhere with absolutely nothing. What better student could there be than me?

But Thoreau is gone and I'm alone, staring through the trees as a pale yellow haze begins to light the sky at the edge of Walden Pond. The wind rattles some dry leaves in the oak tree above my head, and it sounds a whole lot like laughing.

6

PAST THE CHILL, BEYOND THE SMELL OF DECAYING LEAVES and pine and the fresh mist of morning on Walden Pond, a man's deep voice reaches into my sleep. I'm outside under the sky and I hear his voice. It's not the ghost of Thoreau this time. The voice is more familiar.

Wake up, the voice says. *It's time to gather wood for the fire and make breakfast. We've got a long hike ahead of us today.*

I smile. So happy to be here with him. He calls me by the name I can't remember, and I can almost hear it, the shape and lilt of my forgotten name.

"Dad?"

A man clears his throat awkwardly. "Uh. Excuse me. I don't think you're supposed to be here."

My head jerks toward the man's voice, and I pull a stiff muscle in my neck with a twang. Some big guy with a black goatee stands looking down at me, clutching a crooked walking stick.

"The park isn't open yet," he tells me.

"What? Oh, sorry." My voice is thick with sleep, and my mouth feels full of marshmallows. Just the sight of his leather jacket and black wool hat makes me shiver, jealous of the warmth. I sit up, fighting grogginess, and rub the stiff place in my neck.

As he stares at me, I imagine my wild hair with leaves poking out of it, my wrinkled clothes and sleep-creased face. Surely he can see I'm merely pathetic and not a threat.

Leaning on his stick with one hand hitched up on his hip, he asks, "Did you sleep here all night?"

I scratch my head and pull an oak leaf out of my hair. "I wouldn't call it sleeping, exactly."

He smiles, which makes friendly creases around his eyes. "Well, just so you know, Walden Pond doesn't officially open until seven a.m." He pulls back a coat sleeve to consult his watch. "And it's about six forty-five at the moment."

My forehead crunches into a frown. What? Can they actually close the pond? Close the woods? I wonder if he's going to arrest me. With his bulky build and shrewd, guarded expression, he could be a cop. Or maybe an ex-con. I want to ask what he's doing here if the pond is closed, but I don't want to sound like a smartass.

"I work for the park commission, and I come here for my morning walks," he explains, as if reading my thoughts. "I'm a Thoreau interpreter," he adds, like he's expecting me to be impressed.

I stand up and brush pine needles off the sleeve of my sweater. "You…translate his writing into other languages?"

He stares at me, then a chuckle erupts from somewhere deep in his wide chest. "No, not that kind of interpreter. I'm a historic interpreter. I pose as Thoreau, wear the kind of clothes he would have worn, make appearances and give talks. That kind of thing. People ask questions and I answer as Thoreau. It's fun."

I narrow my eyes at his tall, muscular body, trying to imagine him in an outfit like Thoreau's. He doesn't look anything like the short, thin version of Thoreau I saw— dreamed, hallucinated, whatever—but he seems like a nice guy so I don't want to hurt his feelings.

He takes a deep breath of morning air, and looks out at the misty lake reflecting the sun. *"A morning walk is a blessing for the whole day,"* he says. I recognize the quote. Thoreau, of course.

"*Only that day dawns to which we are awake*," I quote back automatically, stifling a yawn.

The man laughs. "Clever," he says. "Very clever. By the way, my name's Thomas." He extends a hand. I try to muster a decent grip inside his paw of a hand.

"I'm Hank."

As soon as he takes my hand, Thomas yanks his back in surprise. "Christ, Hank. Your hands are like ice." For the first time, he notices that I'm shivering my ass off. He stares at me, trying to figure me out.

"You need a ride home, Hank?" he asks.

Home. "Uh, no thanks." I stuff my hands into my pockets and stare at the ground. When I glance up again at Thomas's face, I see kindness.

"Well at least let me help you get warmed up. I have hot coffee in a thermos and a couple bagels back at my vehicle. I'd be happy to share them with you."

I squint into the morning sun behind his head and say, "Sure," trying to sound casual. But I'm suddenly feeling so grateful that I have to swallow the lump in my throat.

After crossing the street with Thomas, I spot Thoreau's cabin. The cabin isn't on the hill by Walden Pond where it belongs, but all the way over here, practically in the parking lot.

"Why is the cabin *here*? It doesn't belong here," I say, pissed. If I'd only known last night that it was here all along, so close.

Thomas stands with his keys in one hand. "It's a replica," he tells me. "The actual cabin was moved and collapsed years ago. So they built this one from old photos and descriptions in Henry's book."

A replica. I walk closer, peer in the window.

"Do you want to go in?" Thomas smiles at me. "I have the key. It's time to open for the tourists anyway. "

"Yeah, I would."

"First let me grab breakfast." He jabs a thumb toward a motorcycle parked about twenty feet in front of us, black and chrome, reflecting the morning sun. A historian with a Harley. If that historian was anybody else, it might seem strange. But somehow, it fits Thomas. I watch as he saunters over to the bike in his black boots, opens a compartment in the back, and takes out a backpack.

Inside the cabin, it's just the way I imagined it when I read the book, almost exactly the way it looked in my dream. A bed. A desk and table, painted green.

"Three chairs," I say, unconsciously quoting Henry again. "*One for solitude, two for friendship, three for society.*"

Thomas lifts his eyebrows. "That's exactly right." He sets his walking stick in a corner and sits in the chair closest to the fireplace. He takes a thermos out of the backpack and pours steaming coffee into a plastic mug, which he offers to me. I cup my hands around its warmth.

"So, they lock this place up at night?" I ask casually and sit on the edge of the bed. The mattress crackles under me, like it's filled with straw. The coffee is black and tastes bitter but warms me from the inside out, so I don't mind.

"Of course. Concord's a nice town, but they can't leave it open." Thomas takes off his leather jacket and drapes it over the back of the chair. "Some vagrant might show up and try to sleep here."

I nod sympathetically. "Yeah." Some vagrant. Like me. I examine the windows, wondering how hard it might be to jimmy one open.

Thomas hands me a buttered bagel in a plastic bag. I rip the bag open and eat too fast, realizing I haven't had food since yesterday afternoon on the train from New York.

"Hungry?" Thomas takes a civilized bite into his own bagel and smiles.

"Growing boy," I say with my mouth full, but try to take smaller bites so I won't look like a total pig.

Thomas pours me more coffee. "Well, you look better now than you did when I first saw you this morning." He reaches over and picks up my copy of *Walden* from where I'd set it next to me on the bed and flips it to the back, to the photograph of Thoreau with his pale-eyed, serious expression. "You looked like you fell out of the sky or something."

Wiping my buttery fingers off on my jeans, I hope I don't look like too much of a slob. When I glance up at Thomas, he's not looking at the book anymore, but intently at me.

"So where did you come from, Hank?"

I shrug, feeling slightly buzzed from too much caffeine and too little sleep. "I guess I fell out of the sky or something." Why not? It's as good an explanation as any. And even though Thomas has been kind to me, I decide not to tell him the truth. There are still so many questions I need to answer for myself first.

"I see you value your privacy, and I respect that," Thomas says, looking down at his hands. "But come on, I have to ask. Why were you sleeping outside at the cabin site? Don't worry, you're not in trouble. I'm just curious."

"Well," I say reasonably. "I wouldn't have been sleeping outside if the cabin had been there like it was supposed to be."

Thomas smirks. "Fair enough."

I stand and nonchalantly try to open one of the windows, like I just want some air, and all I manage to do is disturb a spider, who scuttles to a corner of his web. The window is nailed shut. Figures. Outside, instead of a view of trees and bushes that should be there, there's a view of the parking lot and the road, where rush hour cars are whizzing by. Not the best location for a hideout.

"It's not right," I say, half to myself. "It doesn't belong here."

"I'm sure Henry would agree with you," says Thomas. He reaches up to scratch the back of his head. That's when I notice a design in black ink on his upper arm, showing under the left sleeve of his navy blue T-shirt.

"What's the tat?" I ask.

He pulls up his sleeve to show me the tattoo of a man's face in profile, a man with an old fashioned black beard. Under it is written in fancy script lettering like a signature: "Henry D. Thoreau."

"You know." I pause, uncertain how to say what I'm thinking. "I hope you don't mind me saying this, but—"

"But I don't act like a stodgy Thoreau-loving historian-slash-scholar who works for the park commission?"

"Something like that."

"Yeah, I know. I get that all the time." He gets up, screws the top on his thermos and gathers the remains of our breakfast. "I'm heading into town. Want a ride?"

A ride on the Harley? Hell, yeah. We head out to the parking lot and walk to the motorcycle. "For a kid who worships Thoreau enough to stay all night at his cabin site, you have a lot to learn," Thomas says, handing me a spare helmet from the back of his bike. "Thoreau was a rabble-rouser in his time. A free spirit. A rebel." He pulls on his own helmet, straddles his bike, and flashes straight white teeth. "Why do you think I like him so much?"

After Thomas drops me off in town, I aimlessly walk the streets of Concord with my hands stuffed deep into my pockets. I can't stop thinking about seeing Thoreau last night. Sure, it was probably just some freaky dream. But what if it wasn't a dream? What if Thoreau's ghost knows stuff about me and is watching over me like a guardian angel or something? Maybe that's why I woke up with the book next to me at the train station. Maybe it was a sign, a gift from Thoreau himself.

Now that I've had some food to start my day (Essential

Fact of Life Number One), I decide to address Number Two—clothing—at a sporting goods store on Main Street. I buy a warm coat (on sale, half off), plus black sweatpants and a thick gray sweatshirt. I put the sweatpants and sweatshirt on in the dressing room, and stuff the clothes Magpie gave me into the plastic bag. Now I've got two sets of clothes. Nothing fancy, Thoreau wouldn't approve of fancy, but enough to keep me warm.

Next up: shelter.

There is one hotel in town, the Colonial Inn, with a sign outside that says it was built in 1716, but I ask the price at the front desk, and it's way too expensive. My money, Simon's money—*don't think about that*—is dwindling. My shelter has to be safe and it has to be free, someplace where I can stay long enough to get my thoughts together. Just until I remember more about my life and figure out what to do next.

Somehow, I wind up back at the Concord train station, and being there reminds me of meeting Hailey. I think of her smiling green eyes and I get this feeling like, hey, I'd really like to see her again. So I retrace the steps we walked yesterday to the high school. But as soon as I start up the long driveway to the school, I realize something is different. To start with, there are only a few cars in the parking lot. Plus, I don't see any kids outside, playing sports in the fields or sitting on the stone wall. It's a weekend or holiday or something. No school today.

At first I'm disappointed. But then it occurs to me that I need shelter, and here is an entire building comprised of shelter and nobody around. If I can just get inside, there has to be someplace in that big building where a guy could curl up and get some sleep.

I try the front door, but it's locked, so I circle around to the back. Along the side of the building, a red minivan pulls up, and two girls, both with brown hair and pretty faces, pile out of the back seat. Do all the girls in Concord look like perfect little cheerleaders? One of them cuts a glance in my direction with interest but no recognition. They head to a side door, open it, and go inside. I wait a beat or two, and follow them.

Inside, it smells like floor cleaner, sneakers, and pencils. I pass rows of lockers and follow the sounds of the girls talking and giggling, their voices echoing in the empty hallways. When they pass through some double doors, I peek through a small window in one of the doors into the high school auditorium. Rows of red seats face a stage where a group of people are working. Some are standing on ladders with electric drills and hammers, a couple of guys carry in boxes and set them on the side of the stage, and a few girls are painting sets off to one side with black paint. A tall guy with gray dreadlocks, probably the school janitor, pushes a humming vacuum cleaner up the side aisle. He's wearing jeans and a faded tie-dyed T-shirt.

Then I see her. Hailey, sitting on the edge of the stage, swinging her legs back and forth and talking to some guy. *She's here.* Now, instead of wearing her loose lacrosse uniform, she's wearing a tight red sweater and jeans. Her hair is down instead of up in a ponytail, and it's long, curling around her shoulders. Yeah, she looks *hot*.

The guy she's talking to is really into her, gesturing his hands around a lot and talking. I can't tell if she's interested back. He's shorter than me and kind of scrawny, with shaggy brown hair and black jeans. His cap is on sideways and there's a chain attached to his belt, like he thinks he's some suburban punk gangster. Trying to decide whether I should go up and talk to Hailey or just sit in the back of the auditorium, I open the door slowly and slip inside. The heavy door swings shut behind me.

BOOM!

There is a loud cracking sound, and before I can even register what happened, a flash of scrambled images bursts inside my head, metal reflecting twilight. Colors, blue and red, fireworks bursting, a cry like an ice pick in my brain.

I fall to the floor, curl up in a ball, hands over my ears.

"Whoa, buddy. What happened? Did you trip?"

I open my eyes, and a big guy with gray deadlocks and intense blue eyes is staring down at me. After blinking hard for a few seconds, I can finally talk.

"Yeah, I guess so." Foggy, confused. "There was this really loud noise."

"It's that damn door," he says, shaking his head. "I keep trying to fix it, but it needs to be replaced. Every time it slams shut, it's like a bomb went off."

"A crash. Or something," I say.

He looks at me, all curious, but then just nods. "You okay, then?"

"Oh yeah, definitely," I say lightly, though my head is throbbing. He offers a hand to help me to my feet.

Nervously, I glance at the stage, imagining every face turned toward me, staring. But nobody other than the janitor seems to have noticed that I just fell to the floor like I'd been shot in the head.

The janitor nods slowly, as if he's reassuring himself I'm not a lawsuit about to happen. "Okay then. Take it easy." He lifts up the vacuum cleaner with one hand and walks out of the auditorium, keys jangling on his belt.

Sitting in the last row, I wait for my head to stop vibrating, for the gray spots in my vision to clear. Why the hell would the sound of a crashing door cause me to throw myself to the floor like that? Another question without an answer.

I stuff my plastic bag of clothes under the chair in front of me and turn my focus away from my problems and on to the redheaded girl sitting on the stage.

As if sensing my eyes locked on her, Hailey turns and looks up to where I'm sitting, leaning my arms on the seat in front of me, watching her. She squints, and then with one hand, shields her face from the lights on the stage so she can see me better. Encouraged, I stand up and start walking toward her.

Hailey hops off the stage and we meet in the aisle. She looks happy to see me.

"Hank," she says, and gives me this sweet, shy smile. "What are you doing here?"

"I, uh, well, my dad is in town, looking at houses and property and stuff, and I didn't feel like going along. I went for a walk and ended up here." These lies come so easy, I'm proud and ashamed at the same time.

"Does that mean you're transferring soon?"

She sounds hopeful, and I wish I could tell her yes. I wish I was a normal person who could go to this school and attend classes and take Hailey to dances and cheer for the Patriots sports teams.

"I might," I tell her. "Although it's so late in the school

year, I might just hang out in Concord and, you know, do stuff on my own."

"Stuff on your own?"

"Like home-schooling. To finish up the year." I shrug and go for a confident smile to back it up.

She turns her head to one side and crinkles her forehead at me like she doesn't get it. I notice that she's wearing two different earrings, a dangly gold musical note in one ear, and a silver G-clef in the other.

"But where are you living, if your parents don't have a house out here yet?"

"Oh, I have this, well, uncle who lives in town. I'm staying with him." All these stacked-up lies are starting to make me nauseous. I gesture toward the stage. "So, what's going on here?"

Hailey looks behind her at the stage. "Oh, it's this thing we do every year called the Battle of the Bands, coming up in a couple weeks. It's a big deal, with sets and lights and fog machines and stuff. A big deal for us, anyway."

"That's cool. You in the show?" I ask.

She looks away, shrugs. "Nah. I'm just helping backstage, organizing and stuff."

From the stage, the suburban gangster is staring at the two of us.

"That your boyfriend?" I jut my chin toward the kid.

Startled, Hailey follows my gaze. "Cameron? No. He lives next door to me and we've known each other since we were kids. That's all." She shrugs. "Well, I should get back to work. Stick around for a while if you want."

"Sure. Can I help?" I ask her.

Hailey introduces me to this hyper blond lady named Ms. Coleman who's obviously in charge of the event. "This is Hank, he's a new student here," Hailey says, cutting me a look that says, *just go with it.* "Can he help out?"

"Of course, of course," Ms. Coleman says. She's so busy she barely even looks at me. "Welcome aboard." She points out a toolbox and gives some vague directions about building sets.

For about an hour, I join the other kids (who ignore me for the most part, which is fine with me), working on the sets and trying to be helpful. It turns out I'm good with my hands, adept at drilling into wood frames and thinking through how things should fit together. Building stuff comes naturally to me. My hands remember. Maybe my dad taught me.

Then I recall the voice I heard in the woods this morning, calling me. It wasn't Thoreau and it wasn't Thomas either. It was my father. I know this. Although I can't conjure a picture of him in my head, at least there's no warning slash in my gut when I try.

"Hey, you." There's a voice coming from somewhere above my head. I glance up to see Cameron standing on a platform above the stage. "Can you bring up that spotlight for me?"

He points to a black unit by my feet, with metal flaps in front of a large bulb, and a loop on top like a handle. "Sure." It's heavier than it looks. The only way up to the platform is a makeshift ladder, blocks of wood nailed into the wall. With one hand carrying the spotlight, the other grasping the ladder, I climb up to where Cameron is kneeling at the edge of the platform. It's hard to stand there and lift up the light without losing my balance, but I manage.

Cameron waits a beat longer than necessary to reach out for the light, like he's hoping maybe, just maybe, I'll slip and fall. I see it in his eyes. He reaches to lift the spotlight out of my hands, but just as I'm letting go, he releases his grip and the weight of it comes down on me. Asshole. Instinctively, I reach for the spotlight with both hands, afraid to let the unit go crashing to the floor, and I almost fall backward off the ladder. Just in time, Cameron grabs my arm. "Sorry," he says, not looking in the least bit sorry. "Lost my grip."

I smirk at him, drilling into him with my own unflinching eye contact. "Yeah, right." I say.

He turns away from me to hang the spotlight, standing on a narrow catwalk and reaching up into the black-painted rafters. The platform at the top of the ladder is not a big area, just about the same size as Thoreau's cabin. Still, there's enough space for a guy to stand and hang lights. Or hide.

"Okay, good work, everybody," Ms. Coleman calls out. "We've made a lot of progress. Let's clean up and have some lunch."

In the kitchen, there are boxes of pizza somebody ordered for the cast and crew. I feel awkward around the other kids, like an intruder, but the last thing I'd do in my situation is refuse free food. So I take a couple of slices of pepperoni and chow down. The other kids sneak glances at me, but nobody talks to me. Fair enough. I don't try to start a conversation either. It's hard to talk to people when I'm a stranger, not just to them, but to myself.

I look for Hailey, but Cameron has taken her aside, doing his possessive act again, telling her some long involved story (she keeps looking in my direction; am I only imagining she wants me to rescue her?), so I casually slip out of the kitchen.

With nothing better to do, I wander into an open room adjoining the auditorium. There are music stands, lockers, instruments, and random pieces of sheet music scattered on the floor. The band room. And there in a corner, somebody has left an acoustic guitar. It's not a fancy or expensive guitar, just a dusty old Yamaha, but for some reason, I'm drawn to it. I pick it up, run my fingers over the wood on the neck. Placing my fingers on the top frets, I play a D chord, and wince when I hear how out of tune it is. So I twist the pegs, get it in tune, and start playing a song I don't recognize, but my fingers seem to remember by heart.

Now *this* is cool. I know how to play guitar. Music, as it turns out, feels as natural to me as breathing. Feels so good, I forget where I am. Close my eyes, let my fingers fly, and play the hell out of that old guitar.

At first I think I'm imagining things when I hear singing. But I open my eyes, and there's Hailey, leaning against the lockers.

"No, Hank, keep playing," she says. "I love the Beatles. My mom played their stuff all the time when I was little."

So the song I'm playing is something by the Beatles. A spark of memory snaps into place, like synapses repairing themselves. The Beatles. Of course.

I try to start the song again, but I'm flustered and forget how to play, unable to pick up where I left off. Then I make myself relax, return to that place where my fingers did the remembering. It comes back, and Hailey sings. She has a gorgeous voice, silky but with this raspy quality that makes it unique. Sexy. Here and there I miss a chord because I'm distracted by her singing, and she misses a few words, but while we're playing, I feel like I'm on a different planet. A planet where only Hailey and I exist, like we've been making music together forever.

And as she sings, I listen to the lyrics and remember the name of the song. "Blackbird."

The last notes of "Blackbird" hang in the air for a while after we're done, and I hold my breath. "Wow," I say at last. "You have the most amazing voice."

She looks away from me then, shrugs. "I dunno," she murmurs, but I can tell she's trying not to smile.

"So explain to me why you're not performing in the Battle of the Bands."

Hailey plays with the zipper on her red sweater. "Couldn't get a band together. I mean, I did it last year, but it didn't work out this time."

"When is the show?"

"Two weeks."

"That's enough time to pull your band back together, isn't it? Maybe I can help." Call me delusional, call me impulsive, whatever, but under the new influence of music, I feel like anything is possible. Plus, I'd grab any excuse to spend more time with this girl. There's just something about her.

"I don't know," Hailey says. She won't look at me. "Last year, there was this thing. But look, it's no big deal. We can talk about this later. Even if we don't enter the competition, we can play together for fun if you want. You still have my number, right?"

"Yes," I say. "I'll call you. Definitely."

She nods and smiles this cool, really pretty smile. "I'd like that. Thanks."

I set the guitar back in the corner, and together, we head back down the hallway and into the auditorium.

Later, I stand inside the front lobby of the school with the rest of the kids, pretending to watch for my parents' car pulling up in front of the school to fetch me. After Hailey leaves, giving me a wave and flashing that dimple, I excuse myself to go to the boys' room, but nobody seems to hear me, or even notice I've slipped away. Perfect. I hang out in the bathroom until all is quiet, and I'm pretty sure the last kid has left.

Blending into the hollow silence of the school, I set out to explore. Walking down the empty hallways is kind of creepy, like being the last person left alive after a nuclear attack. But then I start thinking, hey, if there was a nuclear attack and I was the sole survivor, everything I need to keep myself alive is right here at Henry David Thoreau Regional High School.

Clothing? All set. Not just the clothes I already own, but when I investigate the boys' locker room, I find a big cardboard box shoved up against a wall in the corner, marked *Lost and Found*. It's full of T-shirts and gym shorts, collared shirts and jeans, even sneakers and jackets, and some look like they're my size. How rich are the kids in this town that they can completely forget to bring home all these clothes? I'm sure Thoreau would have plenty to say about that.

As for food, the cafeteria has all the food I can eat, if I can get past the locked door. Through the window in the kitchen door, I see enormous cans of food like applesauce, tomato sauce, and peaches stacked on the counters. I'd never go hungry.

Turning away from the kitchen door, I'm trying to figure out where I can lie down and get some sleep. All the classroom doors are locked, the nurse's office is locked, the library is locked. I'm thinking maybe the best I can do is head back to the auditorium and try to curl up in one of those red seats, when a woman in a plaid flannel shirt and jeans comes bursting out of a closet clutching a mop. We collide right into each other and she tumbles backward, landing on her butt on the floor. The keys attached to her belt loop make a jangling crash, and the mop goes flying.

"Oh man. I'm so sorry," I say, reaching over to help her to her feet.

"Excuse me," she says, wide eyes startled. She has gray-streaked hair in frizzy curls past her shoulders, but her face looks young somehow. Innocent.

Once she's on her feet again, I get the mop and hand it back to her. "Are you all right?"

The woman stares at me for a long moment, narrowing her eyes. "Michael?" she whispers.

My heart lurches. *Do you know me?* I search for something familiar in her thin face. She's sort of pretty in an all-natural, former-hippy kind of way.

"I'm sorry." She shakes her head as if she's trying to wake up from a weird dream. "You look like somebody I knew once," she says.

Michael. I examine the name, repeat it in my head, but feel no spark of recognition.

Heavy footsteps approach, then a man's voice interrupts. "You still here, kid?" Turning, I see the dread-locked janitor. His intense eyes snap at me with intelligence and suspicion.

"Well, I—I was helping out with sets, and my dad hasn't come for me yet. Can you tell me where there's a phone so I can call him?"

"You don't have a cell phone?" he asks. "I thought all you kids had phones."

"I don't have one at the moment. It…broke, and I don't have my new one yet." With his unflinching gaze on me, my lies seem completely transparent.

"There's a pay phone by the front door," he says. "You never noticed?"

"I never noticed," I say lightly in what I hope is a charming way. That's when I see something shimmering on the cafeteria floor, where it skittered under a chair. It's a set of keys. They must have fallen off the janitor's belt loop when she fell. I rip my eyes away from the keys, hoping the janitors won't notice.

The woman clears her throat softly behind me. "Billy," she says. "Doesn't he look a lot like Michael?"

Billy's expression softens when he looks at the woman. "Maybe a little. Around the eyes. But come on, Sophie, we need to finish up. Some kid puked in the back hallway." He cuts a resentful look in my direction, as if he suspects me. "As soon as we get it cleaned up, we can get out of here."

I wonder if the two janitors are a couple. Billy and Sophie, lovers and high school custodians. Michael's parents?

Sophie opens the closet next to the kitchen, takes out a huge wash pail on wheels, and pushes the handle into Billy's hands.

Please don't notice the keys on the floor. Please don't notice the keys.

"I was just leaving," I say to them both. "Have a good one."

With one last wistful look at me, Sophie follows Billy down one of the long hallways, and I head toward the front door. I put the heavy black phone to my ear and pretend to make a call.

Once the two janitors disappear, I set the phone quietly in the cradle and slip back into the kitchen, making sure my sneakers don't squeak on the clean tile floor. With an eye on the cafeteria door, I reach for the keys under the plastic orange seat of the chair. Scoop them up, muffle the jingle, and stuff them into the front pocket of my jeans.

Then I slip noiselessly into the auditorium and ease the door shut slowly, so it won't make that crashing sound. Grabbing my bag of clothes from the place where I tucked it under the seats earlier, I hurry toward the stage. Imagining I hear a sound like maybe a tall janitor wielding a large mop, I scale the ladder to the upper platform in seconds.

Curling up on my side, I make a pillow of the clothes Magpie gave me and a blanket of my coat. I stay there on the platform until my heart rate slows down, until the building grows dark around me with the setting sun. Until I fall asleep.

7

SCUFFING THROUGH THE DEAD LEAVES AND PINE NEEDLES at the side of the road, I head back to Walden Pond the next morning. I'm drawn there, like maybe this is the place where I can find some answers. Which is tough, considering I'm not even sure of the questions.

Last night I slept like a dead person on the stage platform at the school, and woke up in the same position I went to sleep in, my back stiff and no dreams to remember. With Sophie's keys giving me free reign of the school, I took a shower in the boys' locker room and picked out a change of clothes from the lost and found—faded jeans and a long-sleeved black T-shirt. In the cafeteria fridge, I found some ham and cheese sandwiches, milk, and an apple.

My side hurt and was bleeding again, so I let myself into the nurse's office to get antiseptic and bandages. The cut should be better by now, but it's still red around the edges and hurts to touch it. Worst of all, it reminds me of Simon.

In my imagination Simon is a zombie, withered hands reaching, eyes glazed, blood streaking down his forehead, nubby teeth grinning. Will he be looking for me too, like Magpie and those guys who work for him? But no, none of them can find me here. There's no way.

Don't think about it.

Walden Pond is a mirror, reflecting gray-blue skies, the pines, and oak trees with new leaves pushing out of fat buds. Some people are out hiking, but the deeper I go into the woods, the more alone I am. Walking faster, I break into this little trot, a comfortable jogging pace that just feels good. Maybe I really did run track in my former life, because running feels as natural as walking, as playing guitar, as breathing. Somehow I'm even able to set aside the pain in my side to focus on the running. My legs and breaths settle into a rhythm that calms every cell in my body like meditation, like some kind of drug. Even though my body is moving, my mind is relaxed.

A collage of images floats into my consciousness, snapshot memories of Jack and Nessa, of Magpie and

Simon. Thomas. There's Hailey smiling at me and Cameron glaring. Ms. Coleman. Sophie and Billy. In such a short time, my weird disjointed life has put me in contact with a lot of people. Some I'm glad to have etched on my brain. Others I'd erase in a nanosecond if I could figure out how.

Leaves and pebbles and pine needles crunch in cadence under my sneakers, lulling me into a comfortable trance, and in this frame of mind, I try to access the memories that lie just out of reach.

Gently pressing my memory to the edge of places that don't feel safe, I think: *Dad.* Then I think: *Mom.* The beast inside twitches in its sleep, but I refuse to surrender, focusing instead on my pumping arms and legs, my breaths. Inhale. Exhale.

Dad. Mom.

Like a camera taking a picture, an image of my dad flashes behind my eyeballs. Tall man, dark hair, wire rimmed glasses, gray eyes like mine, a kind smile. We are outside, Dad and me. We're in the woods, building a fire. We have sleeping bags and backpacks and compasses. This is something we do together, something that belongs to us.

Now I see Dad clutching a suitcase, waving good-bye. There are no words, but I know he is going, leaving again. My heart clenches like a fist. Don't go, Dad.

I almost trip over a fallen branch on the trail, but as I regain my footing, another image floats into my consciousness. Mom. Hair blond and wavy, face anxious and thin, a half-empty glass of red wine clutched in her hand as she stares out a window. Doesn't look at me, doesn't see me. I yell something at her, then turn and charge out a blue door with a half-circle window. I slam it shut, the window shatters, and glass skitters on the floor, but she doesn't even turn around.

My breath hitches in my chest, but I press my memory even further, contemplate another word: *sister*.

The beast roars awake as if I poked it with a stick and I completely lose the rhythm of running and breathing. Stumble off the path into a small inlet next to the pond, hidden from the path by a hill and a cluster of evergreens. Leaning against a tree branch, wheezing, I peer into the green-brown water of Walden Pond.

Searing pain blinds me and I grab my head to keep it from exploding, forcing myself to go there again. *Sister.* The thing inside expands, rips at the lining of my stomach, squeezes my lungs. *Sister.* It's trying to kill me, wants me dead. Better dead than to remember.

My legs are rubber, give out, and I collapse on a big rock, doubled over to cradle my seizing stomach. My

God. My entire body drifts toward unconsciousness, and I'm falling. No. Can't let myself pass out. Have to remember.

Sister.

Too close to the edge of the rock, I slip on a sludge-coated corner and tumble forward into the water, shatter the smooth surface, and go under. Cold water seeps into my hair, my clothes and shocks me to my core. I float, stunned and weightless under the green water, at the edge of unconsciousness. The cold seeps into my skin, legs, arms, ears, internal organs, the roots of my hair. But still I float, serene, not even trying to kick my feet or pull toward the surface.

The water is shallow, no danger, not really. And yet. Deep enough. A calm feeling spreads through my veins like water warmed by a secret hot spring. Drowning would be so easy, so sweet.

Then a strange image flashes behind my eyeballs. Open music box, tinny music playing, plastic ballerina twirling. And then I see her. My sister. Big blue eyes, long eyelashes. Yellow-white hair, pink shirt, one pink sneaker. The music box grinds to a halt, ballerina twisted to one side, broken. And there is blood. My sister's screams fill my head, jar me from my peaceful drifting.

Save her.

Jamming my feet down, I find the pond's spongy bottom and push myself to the surface, where I fill my lungs with cool fresh air and cough and cough.

I take the long way back to the high school, through the woods, away from the streets. My teeth are chattering and my body is shivering so hard it hurts. Icy pond water squishes in my sneakers with every step and my cold, drenched clothes weigh about fifty pounds, or at least it seems like it. By the time I get there, it's afternoon and the school is already growing dark and silent under clouds threatening rain.

Opening the back door of the school with Sophie's keys, I'm thinking of warm, dry clothes from the lost and found and a hot shower in the boys' locker room. But then I'm stopped short by a shrill beeping sound. It's coming from the keypad on the wall near the door, which flashes the words *enter code* in a small gray screen.

Oh crap. Even though I opened the outside door with the key, there's some kind of backup security system that needs a code. Just a few numbers punched in, that's all. In a panic, I pound a few keys, as if somehow randomly I'll hit the right combination. Stupid. After about thirty seconds, it's all over. The burglar alarm starts screaming, a continuous, pulsing wail. The police are probably on their way.

I run down the hall, toward the auditorium to my hiding place above the stage. Just in time, I realize I'm leaving wet footprints behind me. The pond water is squishing out of my sneakers leaving a trail. I duck into the boys' room, where I take off my wet sneakers, my wet clothes, and quickly dry off with paper towels. Then I wad up more paper towels, rush back into the hallway and do my best to dry the footprints, pushing the towels around with my feet. I run back to my hiding place, dressed only in my underwear, clothes bunched in my arms.

Just as I'm scrambling up to the platform above the stage, the sound of a door forced open echoes down a long hallway. There are low murmurs, voices I can't make out. Abruptly, the alarm is silenced, leaving my ears ringing as I huddle in a ball, shivering. I'm terrified that I left footprints leading to my hiding place; sure they'll hear my heavy breathing and the jack-hammer of my heart.

Disembodied voices and footsteps echo through the school. Approaching, closer. Too afraid to peer down into the auditorium space, I try to slow my breaths. Two men are here. I hear their voices.

"Just a false alarm, Terry. Second time this month. Everything seems secure."

"Well, hold on," says the cop named Terry. In moments, his footsteps echo on the wooden stage. I can see the beam of a flashlight, sweeping the stage. Can he hear me breathing? I cringe, motionless. Then I hear the drip.

The wet pile of clothes next to me is dripping through the spaces between the platform boards. Water plops gently to the floor below.

Eyes shut tight, I wait for the officer to shout orders at me, or climb up to get me, handcuffs ready to snap on my wrists.

"Terry, come on, there's nothing here."

"There's a little water here on the floor," the cop says. I imagine the flashlight examining the puddle, then sense its beam sweeping up to my hiding place above his head. I hold my breath.

"Just a leak," he murmurs. Then louder he says, "Okay, Jim, let's go. Everything checks out."

I'm still holding my breath as I follow the sound of their footsteps on the hollow stage and then disappearing down the hall. Finally, I let the air out of my lungs with a low hiss, but I'm still too terrified to move. I stay there for a long time to reassure myself they're really gone, until my trembling knees and elbows make knocking sounds on the wood.

Still dressed only in my underwear, I go into the boys' locker room and start a shower, let the room fill with steam and stand motionless under the hot water until the cold leaches out of my body.

I pull on dry clothes from the lost and found—a striped shirt missing a button, baggy jeans, and sneakers about a half-size too big. I focus on these tasks, even though my entire body hums with restlessness.

All I can think about now is my sister in danger, blond hair, pink sneaker, and too much blood. Big eyes so scared. If I thought it would help, I'd be sprinting down the streets of Concord now to get to her. But that would accomplish nothing. First, I don't know how to find her. Second, my body is weak, exhausted, depleted. I can hardly even think.

Only one true, clear thought slices through my exhaustion: I have to find out who I am, so I can figure out how to get to her. This is not about me anymore. Even the beast can't keep me from her or prevent me from remembering more. I won't let it.

For now though, my mind and body are numb. Just need to get warm. Just need to rest. Build up my strength so I can focus on finding her.

Using Sophie's keys, I let myself in the nurse's office to put fresh bandages on my side. It hurts more than before, and now there's yellow pus oozing out of the cut. The red skin around the cut is hot, and my face feels hot too. At the same time, there's this chunk of ice inside me. So cold. I find blankets on a cupboard shelf, lie shivering on one of the cots, and the tide of sleep takes me under in a heartbeat.

❧

"Time to wake up, son."

A voice jolts me from a dream, and my eyes fly open to see a woman sitting in a chair like she's been there a while, watching me sleep. Gray-streaked, curly hair. Young-old face with sad brown eyes. It takes a moment to recognize the janitor.

"You're not supposed to be in here, you know." Her voice is firm, but also kind.

"I'm sorry," I say politely, as if I've taken a wrong turn and wandered by accident into her fancy rose garden. "I'll go." My temples pound when I sit up.

But she just sits there, head cocked to one side like she's in no hurry for me to leave. "It really is amazing how much you look like Michael."

"Michael is…your son?"

Sophie nods, focusing dry eyes on the medicine cabinet over my shoulder. "He died a few years ago, when he was thirteen. Leukemia. But I bet he'd look a lot like you now. What are you, seventeen? Eighteen?"

"Um, yeah."

"By the way, I also know you're not a student here." She frowns at me, but she doesn't actually seem angry. "You're lucky Billy isn't good at remembering faces like I am. You're trespassing on town property."

"I'm sorry," I say again. For some reason, I can't lie to this woman who watched me sleep and called me by her son's name.

"So, tell me. What are you doing in the nurse's office at six in the morning when nobody but the janitors are supposed to be here?"

"I'm here, because—" A hundred lies pass through my head and I discard them all. "I'm here because I ran away from home and there's no place else to go."

Her face is soft and sad as she reaches out to touch my cheek. Her fingers are ice cold against my skin, and I flinch. "You're feverish," she says with such deep concern that all I want is to lie on this cot and let this nice lady take care of me so I can feel better and find my sister.

The distant sound of a man whistling off-key echoes

down the hallway. "There's Billy," says Sophie. She rises to her feet and peers down at me. "You need to go. Even if I wanted to let you stay, I can't. I'd lose my job."

"I understand," I say.

Reaching out a finger, she brushes hair out of my eyes. "What's your name?" she asks me.

"Hank."

"Hank, call your mother," she whispers, like she knows something about me that I don't. "I guarantee she would sacrifice her own life just to have you back home. Understand?"

I nod, my eyes burning. She turns toward the door, clears her throat, and asks, "By the way, you didn't come across a set of keys the other night, did you?"

I don't even try to sidestep the question. Instead, I reach into my pocket and give her an apologetic smile as the keys chink into her open hand.

"Good boy," she says, and she leaves the room. The words float in her wake, and something inside me longs to follow after her. But I just lie there and listen as her footsteps echo down the hallway and disappear.

8

IT'S EARLY MORNING IN DOWNTOWN CONCORD, BUT already the entire town seems wide awake. Sitting near the window inside the doughnut shop, I watch normal citizens go about their normal lives. Just the start of another day. A line of people snakes out the door, waiting to order their large coffees, doughnuts, and breakfast sandwiches. My coffee is black and I nibble on a double chocolate doughnut. Chocolate for breakfast. I thought it would cheer me up; make things look a little better. It doesn't.

Once again, I'm in search of shelter. It's hard to focus on moving forward in my completely unsettled life when I don't even know where I'm going to sleep tonight.

Plus, I'm running dangerously low on money. Something's got to change soon. A part of me actually considers going back to New York to find Jack and Nessa. At least that way, I wouldn't be so alone. And lonely.

With my teeth I rip open a packet of Advil that I bought at the convenience store across the street, and wash them down with bitter coffee. Maybe if I can get rid of this headache and stop feeling so dizzy, I'll be able to think straight. Like some wounded animal, I want to curl up and hide until I feel better. Even animals can find a cave or a hole in a tree where they can rest. Where can I go?

When the workers behind the counter in their goofy paper hats start giving me funny looks and whispering to each other, I figure I've overstayed my welcome. I hit the streets and just walk. One foot and then the other foot, getting me somewhere. Anywhere. As if they know where they're going, they take me down the street to the Concord Free Public Library. They take me up the stairs and through the front door. Public building. Warmth. Shelter. I'm in.

At first I'm kind of surprised that it's not the Henry David Thoreau Memorial Library. I mean, isn't everything in Concord named after Thoreau? And when I wander into the lobby, I'm sure at first that the life-size white marble statue of a guy sitting on a throne-like chair is Thoreau too. I almost expect him to get up off his marble throne and start yelling at me for being such a failure. But the base of the statue says he's Ralph Waldo Emerson. That name again. Guess he was pretty famous in Concord. One of Thoreau's buddies, maybe. Whatever.

Damn, my head hurts.

"Hank?"

At first I think I've imagined someone saying my name. But when I hear it again, I whirl around and see a big man in black horn-rimmed glasses standing behind me in the library lobby, smiling like he's happy to see me.

I look at him blankly.

"Hank, it's me." When I still don't respond, he pulls off the glasses.

"Thomas?"

He laughs at my stunned expression. "In the flesh. Good to see you, Hank." He reaches out a huge hand to give me a cheerful smack on the shoulder that actually hurts.

"Good to see you," I echo weakly.

"So what brings you to the library in the middle of the morning?"

"I want to take out books," I say. Duh, I sound like a moron.

"Isn't this a school day? Shouldn't you be in school?"

"Well." My mind races, and I remember what I said to Hailey two days ago. "I'm home-schooled, so I do a lot of projects on my own. Today I'm here to do some research for a paper I'm working on."

"Well then, today's your lucky day," Thomas says, flashing straight white teeth. "In addition to being a historian, I'm the research librarian here." He pulls up the right sleeve of his green T-shirt to show me the tattoo of a cobra, coiled and ready to strike. Except that it's wearing a pair of black-rimmed glasses just like Thomas's, and above the snake is one word in fancy Gothic lettering: "Bookworm."

"I can hook you up with any research materials you might need." He settles his black glasses on the end of his nose and sits down at his desk, fingers poised over his computer keyboard. He smiles up at me expectantly. "So."

"So?"

"What's the subject you're researching today?"

My mind chokes, just when I need it to be creative. "Well, I'm working on a paper about…"

My glance drifts around the room, searching for something, anything that might inspire a potential research paper project. Nothing comes to me. Can't think straight. Must be this stupid headache, the heat gathering under my skin, so distracting.

But then, I see them. Perched high on the ends of several bookshelves in the lobby, there's a row of four statues. They're carved in white marble like the Emerson one, except these are just the heads and shoulders of people, like the tops of their bodies were hacked off and set on pedestals.

"…famous people who lived in Concord. Since I'm new to the town and all, I thought it would be an interesting and educational subject for me to pursue."

Lame, lame, lame. There's no way Thomas is going to buy that. But I don't seem capable of coming up with anything better. Thomas looks skeptical as he peers at me over his glasses, which I totally deserve, but then his glance follows mine, up to the statues.

"You mean, like those dudes up there?"

I offer a non committal nod-shrug combo.

"Actually, that's a really good place to start." Thomas is such a huge history geek that he warms up to the subject immediately and starts telling me who each of the people are, but I'm having trouble concentrating. The guy who looks like he's sitting on a throne is Ralph Waldo Emerson, who was a big-shot writer in his day. One of the statue heads is Ephraim somebody, and he created the Concord grape. That's his claim to fame. Another head is Louisa May Alcott who mostly wrote books for girls. Then there's Ebenezer who was a judge and whose last name is Hoar. I bet he got teased a lot in high school for that. When Thomas starts rambling on about the statue of Bronson Alcott, who was Louisa May's dad and started some fancy progressive school or something, my eyes start to glaze over. I hope Thomas doesn't notice. "And, of course, over here, is our friend Henry Thoreau."

Thomas points to another pedestal off to his right, away from the other statues. On it is another one of those head-and-shoulder deals, but this time it's Thoreau. I take a closer look, stare into those empty white statue eyes. I don't remember him having such a huge nose.

"They all knew each other in Concord in the mid-nineteenth century and moved around in the same circles. I'll look for one book of biographies that deals with all of them if you want," Thomas says.

"Yeah, sure. That would be great."

He leans over his computer screen, starts tapping away at the keyboard, and then jogs over to a nearby shelf to grab a book. Sitting back down at his desk, he leafs through it and attaches a yellow sticky note to each page that corresponds to one of the statue people. Then he hands the book to me like it's the fricking Holy Grail.

"Thanks, man," I say.

Thomas nods at me, all pleased with himself, but then takes a good long look at me and yanks off his glasses. "You feeling okay, Hank?" he asks me. "Your eyes look a little glassy."

"Nah, I'm okay," I tell him. "Just not getting enough sleep, I guess."

"You're not still sleeping at Walden, are you?" he asks in a low voice.

I force a laugh. "Of course not. That was just one of those things. Just that one crazy night."

Thomas nods thoughtfully. "The night you fell out of the sky."

"Yeah." I clear my throat, shuffle a bit, and pick up the book. "Thanks for this," I tell him. "I'll go read it right now."

I duck into the next room, where there are tables and chairs for studying. I sit at a round table near the window, and scan the biographies of all the statue people in the book, including Emerson and Thoreau, just in case Thomas decides to grill me about them. But my head hurts so badly, it's hard to focus. So when I'm done, I get up, cram all my stuff, including the library book,

into my lost-and-found backpack, and do some exploring.

Down the hall, I find the men's room. Pulling up my shirt in the stall, I can see the pus from my cut oozing through the bandage, even though I just changed it. The damn thing is throbbing and hurts like hell. So I change the bandage again, using fresh supplies I took from the nurse's office before I left the school.

Continuing my scouting mission, I discover the library has three floors of books, plus a basement level with a boardroom and a candy machine. There are a lot of places where a guy seeking shelter could hide for a day or two. I buy myself a package of peanut butter crackers from the machine and eat them for lunch.

Back on the first floor, I sit on the big couch in the lobby next to the statue of Emerson in his chair, and under the watchful eyes of the other statues. Sinking into the comfort of the couch, I pretend to continue reading the library book Thomas gave me, so I won't look like some random homeless person who just wandered into the library to take a nap. Even though that's exactly what I am and exactly what I feel like doing. I close my eyes against the throbbing pain in my head.

"Hank, wake up. The library closes in ten minutes."

"What? Oh. Okay."

Garbled thoughts, twisted and confused, sinking in quicksand, can't think. All I want is to sleep and sleep. I close my eyes again; drift back under.

"Look at me, Hank." This time, Thomas has a hand on my shoulder and is gently shaking me. "You definitely don't look well, my friend."

I force myself to open my eyes wide, though it hurts. Everything hurts, especially my side, where the knife wound is throbbing. "I'm fine," I lie. "Really." Feeling like a drunk person, I peer around at my surroundings, not fully recognizing where I am, not caring. I pick up the library book and hand it back to Thomas. "Thanks. I'll be going now."

I get up, grab my backpack, and sway just a bit on my feet as I take a step toward the door.

"Hank, wait. At least let me make sure you get home."

"No, it's okay." Not looking at him, I adjust the strap of the pack on my shoulder. "My parents should be outside right now to pick me up."

Wanting to believe me, he nods, relief in his dark eyes, like maybe he actually cares what happens to me. A woman enters the lobby and I register dark hair and a blue sweater, but the rest of her is a blur.

"Thomas, I can't get the main computer to shut down," she says. "Something weird keeps popping up on the screen. Can you come take a look?"

"Sure, Annie. I'll be right there." He turns to me and says in a firm voice, "Well, you go home and get some rest now, okay, Hank?"

With a little wave, I pretend to head toward the front door as Thomas leaves the room. But as soon as he's out of sight, I struggle to make my mind work, try to decide where to go, where to hide. What kind of security system would a library have, anyway? Cameras and alarms? Motion detectors?

There's no time to think this through. Next to the couch in the lobby, there's a grand piano, covered with a woven brown cloth that almost reaches the floor. When I hear Thomas's voice rise in the other room, I dive under the piano. By accident, I hit the pedals and the piano makes a muffled, musical bang. I freeze. My heart thumps so loud I imagine it can be heard echoing through the entire library. Cowering, I wait for Thomas to come in and discover my hiding place.

"Come on, let's go already," I hear the woman librarian say to Thomas. "This place gives me the creeps after dark." I hear their footsteps approach the front door. "It's all your fault, you know. All that talk about the library being haunted. I'm going to have nightmares."

Thomas laughs, apparently having forgotten all about me. "Sometimes I swear they're here, especially late at night, trying to communicate with me."

"You *would* think that."

The library goes dark, and I hear the door click shut, locked from the outside, and then all is silent. More silent even than the high school, if that's possible. Silent as a tomb.

I wait a long time, to make sure they're really gone. When I start to get a cramp in my leg, I crawl out from under the piano. I don't need to go far. The couch is right there, inviting me to lie down and sleep. It's too short for my lanky body, but I don't care. I collapse into it, feet trailing over the edge. Just need a good night's rest, and tomorrow will be better. Tomorrow, I'll figure out what to do, how to find my sister. It'll all be better after I sleep.

Just as I start to drift off, there's this strange shushing sound, like the sizzle of the surf. But it gets louder and I recognize what it is. Someone is in this room with me, whispering. What the hell? I open my eyes to see who's here, except that nobody is. I'm alone. Well, almost.

It's the statues. Their lips aren't moving in their frozen marble faces, but I can hear their voices. And after a moment, I can even make out what they're saying.

That guy Ephraim Bull is whispering something like, "Look at me, I'm the Father of the Concord Grape," and Louisa May Alcott is saying, "I wrote *Little Women*, a book beloved by girls all over the world." It reminds me of a boring museum exhibit, or a maybe a video about prominent citizens of nineteenth century Concord, Massachusetts, they'd show kids in middle school. The statues are stiff and without emotion, as if the people they represent were statues too, who never laughed or cried, never got hungry or cold or sick.

"I am Bronson Alcott," whispers the statue with huge eyebrows that look like fuzzy white caterpillars. He mumbles something about this place called Fruitlands he started, which sounds to me kind of like a 1960s commune that didn't work out so well.

Some distant corner of my brain knows this is nothing but a crazy dream, inspired by the book Thomas gave me and brought on by the fever deep-frying my brain cells. But some other part of me is trying to convince me this is real, that the statues really do whisper to themselves in the Concord library at night after everybody goes home.

Ebenezer Hoar's voice grows slightly louder as he states his reason for being memorialized in marble. "I was a judge and a congressman," he says in a bland voice. Big deal. "And if you had appeared in my court, young man, I would have thrown you in prison for the rest of your natural life."

Startled, I glance up at the statue. He is looking straight at me with those spooky white marble eyes without pupils. "And I wager no one would miss you."

The others hiss in agreement, whispers that become threats and I realize there is nothing of the real Alcotts, Judge Hoar, Ephraim Bull, or Ralph Waldo Emerson in these statues at all. And somehow, they seem to know all the dark things about me that I can't remember.

The floor under me starts to shake, and I don't know if the eruption started inside the foundation of the building or someplace deep inside me. The whole library shudders with it, and the statues are silenced as their marble bodies tremble, then quiver toward the edge of their pedestals. Edging closer, closer, then with terrible silent screams, the statues fall one at a time and crash onto the library floor. Not solid marble at all, but with thin exteriors like eggshells that crack open and spew their true contents. Rotting meat crawling with maggots. Fat nightcrawlers and green garter snakes and horned lizards. Broken shards of glass and twisted metal. Razor blades and knives and meat cleavers and spikes. The snakes slither toward me and I can smell rancid flesh.

Henry's statue sits frozen on its pedestal, still intact, watching me with a detached kind of sympathy.

I try to say, *do something, Henry*, but can't make any sound.

Bad spirits rise from the ruins of the statues then, curl toward me and lean over to stare into my face like they can extract information from me or maybe tap into my life force, jealous that their lives are over forever and I'm screwing up mine. They touch my hair and pull at my shirt.

Stop it. I try to swat at their fingers, turn away from their cold breath on my face, but I can't move. *Go away.* Still can't move, can't speak, can't shout, until at last, I can.

🌿

"Get away from me!" Hear my own voice at last, feel my body writhe.

"Shhh. Hank, it's okay, you're all right." Somehow, Thomas is here. Thank God. Thomas. Is here.

"Thomas, make them stop, make them go away."

"There's nobody here, Hank, you're just imagining it. You're burning up with fever, buddy." He has a cell phone in his hand and puts it to his ear. "Help will be here before you know it."

I grab the phone, jab blindly at the Off button, throw it across the room, and scream at Thomas, begging him not to call anyone.

"Jesus, Hank. Calm down. You need help."

But I'm begging, shouting at him like a mental patient. "Don't call, please don't call anybody, you don't understand. Can't let them find me."

"Hank, look at me, open your eyes. Why can't I call someone to help you?"

"My sister."

"Your sister, Hank?"

"My sister needs me, I need to go to her. And I can't help her if I'm in jail."

Thomas rears back. "Jail? What are you talking about, Hank?"

"If you call somebody, they're going to lock me up. Please. I beg you, please, Thomas. Please."

My body heaves with sobs but I'm aware of this from a distance, like I see myself from the ceiling, or maybe I'm one of the statue heads back up on its pedestal, intact and hiding the ugliness inside, looking down and seeing the truth. I'm just a lost boy who has done something too terrible to remember, a trespasser into a world where I don't belong.

Thomas goes quiet, but finally says, "Look, Hank, you can't stay here. The library is opening soon. I'll take you to my house and we'll figure this out. Okay?"

I thank Thomas over and over and he helps me to my feet, wraps one of my arms around his neck and helps me walk outside to his motorcycle. He asks if I'm strong enough to hold on and I say yes, just don't call the cops. We get on the bike and I lean against his wide back trying so hard not to pass out or fall off. And we ride for five minutes or fifty minutes or maybe it's five hours and finally we're at his house and he helps me to his couch and that's all I know.

9

I AM UNDER WATER. AT THE BOTTOM OF WALDEN POND, buried in muck, weighed down by pockets full of rocks. Can't make my way to the surface, but it's okay because it's quiet here. Peaceful. Maybe I'll stay forever.

Now and then I sense people around me, trying to help me, trying to pull me to the surface. They touch my burning face and poke at my side, the place where Simon's knife sliced through my skin, and I scream, but the pond muffles the sound, keeps everything so quiet. It's okay to give in to the quiet. I am safe. Don't have to think about anything, not now. Don't have to remember. Just rest. The remembering can come later. The facing up to things can wait.

Henry stays with me every minute in my underwater sleep, sits on a white rock with his hair floating in the current, and talks to me. He looks a little older than the last time I saw him in a dream. Last time he was clean-shaven, but now he has long sideburns that connect to a full dark beard. Henry helps me pass the time by quoting passages of *Walden* and tests my own twisted memory by having me quote some back. He tells me things about myself. But only the ones I can handle right now, he says. Just little things, like I was obsessed with Legos when I was a kid and my favorite birthday cake was yellow with chocolate frosting. My best friend's name in kindergarten was Silas. But when I ask him to tell me my name, he won't answer. Give it time, he says, just give it all a little time. So I do.

Now and then, a phrase floats in and out of my thoughts. *Old King Cole was a merry old soul and a merry old soul was he.* I thnk its's a song or a poem or something. And it's important somehow. But why? Like the rest of my memories, its significance is always just out of reach.

Underwater there is no time and yet time passes, until I find myself restless with life under the dead leaves and pondweed and invisible jellyfish of Walden. *I think you're ready*, Henry tells me at last, and even though I'm scared to go back, I agree. The sun breaks through the surface of the water, tries to reach me with healing fingers of light. So I kick my feet and push myself back to the air and sunlight and life. Ready now for whatever is next.

***

"Well, look who's back."

Thomas sits in a small wooden chair, big arms resting on his knees, watching me. I'm in a blue-painted bedroom with a slanted ceiling, and the sun shines in the window, too bright. I squint against it, but notice the headache is finally gone. I sit up, too fast, see little bursts of light flashing in front of my eyes, then lean back against a pile of pillows somebody has tucked under my head.

"Whoa, easy, Hank. You're still weak," Thomas says.

I'm wearing a white T-shirt I don't recognize and green plaid pajama pants, probably Thomas's. I lift up the edge of the shirt and see a square of gauze taped onto my skin. When I press on it, it's sore, but not on fire like it was.

"You had a nasty cut there. It got infected and you've been in and out of consciousness for about twenty-four hours," he tells me in a slow, calm voice so I can absorb it all. "I almost gave in and took you to the hospital a couple times, but I figured we'd wait things out if we could. You were really adamant about that. A couple more hours though, and I would've taken you in, no matter what you said."

A woman with short black hair and about six silver earrings in each ear comes into the room and hands a green mug of coffee to Thomas. "Ahh, you're awake," she says with a big smile like she knows me. She's probably thirtyish like Thomas, and pretty in a Goth-lite kind of way. Her hand on my forehead is cool and smells like vanilla. "I figured after the fever broke in the night, you'd be back among the living today."

"Hank, this is Suzanne. She's a friend of mine. And, lucky for both of us, she's also a nurse."

"Hey there, Hank," she says, in this gentle voice exactly like you'd expect from a nurse. "It took a whole lot of antibiotic cream and cold washcloths but we finally got your fever and that nasty infection under control."

Cold washcloths and clothes I don't recognize. My legs twitch. This nurse lady probably saw me naked, and I wasn't conscious enough to remember it. I stare at a tiny diamond stud in the left side of her nose and think about this.

"We considered leeches, but they're hard to come by

this time of year." I can tell Thomas says this to make Suzanne smile and she does, although she rolls her eyes at me like we share a joke.

"So how you feeling, Hank?" she asks. "Kind of like you got hit by a bus?"

I almost say no, it was more like a truck, but all I can do is shrug and nod, like I've forgotten how to speak.

Suzanne pats me on the shoulder like I'm her favorite patient. "You must be starving. Ready to eat something?"

I'm aware of the hollow place in my gut, and find my voice. "Yes. Please."

"Great. I'll see what I can whip up for you in Thomas's kitchen."

We listen to her footsteps descend the wooden stairs.

"Your girlfriend?" I ask Thomas.

He taps a fingernail on the green mug in his big hands, and his face reddens. It's kind of funny—this big, Harley-riding, tattooed guy blushing over a girl. "Maybe. We've kind of bonded over this past day or so. I guess I can thank you for that."

"You're welcome," I say.

Thomas clears his throat, and I know he's holding back, wanting to ask me why I have a knife injury, why I freaked out at the library, why I fell out of the sky and into his life a week ago.

"I just want you to know," he says instead, "that I've been in trouble myself, Hank. When I was younger, I got on the wrong side of the law a couple times and had to learn some lessons the hard way."

He pauses to check my response, but I don't know what to say. I vaguely remember babbling something about jail and begging him not to call the police. But he's going to wonder what kind of trouble I'm in, and I don't know where to start. How can I explain that the trouble that scares me most is the trouble I've forgotten?

"I even did time. A couple years in prison, for breaking and entering." He pauses again. Maybe he's thinking if he opens up to me about his past, I'll do the same. "I'm not proud of it. I was an angry, rebellious kid. I'm still a rebel in my way, but I know how to channel that energy."

Breaking and entering is not as bad as Simon in the alley, assault and battery. Sure, it was self-defense, but would the police see it that way? And there are the crimes I might have committed before I woke up in Penn Station. And there's that other thing. *Maybe you killed somebody.* Did somebody hurt my sister? Did I kill the guy? Is that what I'm blocking out?

"Anyway, I guess I'm just trying to say I understand. And if I can, I'd like to help."

A guitar case is leaning against the wall in a corner of

the room, and I focus on that instead of Thomas. I could use someone to trust. And I could sure use some help. But I'm not ready to ask for it.

"You play guitar?" I ask.

Thomas follows my gaze. He gets the guitar case, brushes away some dust, and lays it at the foot of the bed. He snaps it open, and inside is an old Telecaster with a butterscotch finish, gorgeous and in excellent condition.

"Wow," I say. "Nice ax."

Thomas picks it up, slips the strap over his shoulder, and plays a few licks. It's not plugged into an amp, so the sound is soft and tinny. "Haven't played for a while," he says, twisting the pegs to get it in tune. "But I was in a punk rock group in the nineties. One of the best times in my life." He strokes the body of the guitar like it's a woman and he's madly in love with her. "This guitar helped get me through some really bad stuff, believe me."

"What kind of stuff?" I'd rather talk about music and Thomas than answer any questions about myself.

Thomas runs his fingers up the neck of the guitar, miming chords. "Foster care from the age of eight," he says absently. "Bounced around to four different homes by the time I was eighteen." He clears his throat, then pulls the strap off his shoulder and lovingly puts the guitar back in its red felt-lined case. "Feeling like nobody wants you and you don't belong anywhere can make a person a little crazy," he says.

Uh, yeah.

Just then, Suzanne comes in with a tray, and sets it down on the bed next to me.

"It's just a peanut butter and jelly sandwich and some milk, but Thomas doesn't have much in the way of groceries around here," she says to me. "Not that I'm a gourmet cook or anything, but that's just pathetic."

"I'm a bachelor. I don't need a lot," Thomas says with an easy shrug. "Peanut butter. Jelly. Beer. What else is there?" He latches the guitar case shut and sets it back in the corner.

I'm hungry, so the sandwich tastes incredibly good. And the jelly is grape, which I've decided is my favorite. I'll never be able to eat the stuff again without thinking of that Ephraim Bull guy, father of the Concord grape.

Suzanne goes back downstairs and Thomas and I sit in silence for a couple of minutes, not looking at each other while I eat my sandwich. He jiggles his leg and peers out the window, chewing on a fingernail. Trying to look patient and failing.

"So how did all of that change?" I ask him, licking peanut butter off my thumb.

Thomas stops jiggling his leg and turns toward me. "Excuse me?"

"How did you go from angry to—" I wipe my mouth with a napkin and struggle for the right word. "Not?"

Thomas kicks his feet out in front of him, leans back in his chair, and laces his fingers behind his head. "Well, let's see. After I got out of jail, I drifted around for a while, and finally found a job as a custodian at a library. To stay out of trouble, I spent every free moment there reading everything I could get my hands on. The head librarian was this woman who was impressed that a loser ex-con like me was such a big reader." He frowns and looks out the window, but I notice that Thomas's eyes have grown soft. "She became like a mother to me, made me feel like I belonged somewhere, you know? Long story short, I went to college for American History, got a master's in Library Science, and here I am."

Before I can bombard him with questions to keep him talking, Thomas clears his throat as if placing a period at the end of his story and leans forward in his chair, eyes penetrating mine. "Anyway," he says. "Enough about me."

I stare down at the quilt on the bed until all the colors blend together in a jumbled multicolor blur. "So, I guess it's my turn now," I say. And I realize I really do want to tell him. "First, my name isn't really Hank."

Lying back against the pillows, I tell Thomas everything I know, from the moment I woke up at the train station with *Walden* at my side, not knowing my name or where I came from, to the freak-out scene at the library. I tell him about Simon's knife and the crime I committed in the alley. I tell him about Jack and Nessa and using Simon's money to get a train ticket. Tell him the whole thing in a detached way, like it's somebody else's story, somebody else's life.

Then I tell him about the few memories I can access. Like what I know about my father and mother. My sister. Big eyes, blond hair, blood. That's when it stops feeling like somebody else's story, and it becomes completely and painfully mine.

I have to get out of this bed.

"Hank, take it easy." Thomas is standing by the side of the bed, hand pressing down on my shoulder. "When you're stronger, I'll help you find answers, I promise. I'm a research librarian. Finding answers is what I do, remember?"

I settle back against the feather pillows, letting them engulf me until the dizziness passes. Gazing up at Thomas's strong presence makes a flicker of hope ignite in the center of my chest. But just as quickly, fear snuffs it out.

"Do you think I'll go to jail, Thomas?" Staring up at the ceiling, at water stains and fault-line cracks in the plaster, I feel like a little boy asking if the boogeyman is hiding under my bed. Except that it's way scarier than that. Depending on what I did, somebody like Judge Hoar could send me to jail for the rest of my life.

"I don't know, Hank." Thomas sits down, scratches his shaggy black hair thoughtfully with both hands until it sticks up in spikes. "Your circumstances are unique, so it's hard to say. But look, what you need right now is a safe place to stay for a few days, and you've got that. We'll figure out the rest later."

We. The ceiling cracks and stains blur into amoeba shapes before my watering eyes. "Why would you do this for me?" I whisper.

"Like I told you. When I was younger, some good people helped me out, and that made all the difference," he says. "This is my chance to pay that back. Maybe you'll do the same someday for somebody else."

"Thank you, Thomas." I swallow hard, brush tears from my eyes before they can drip down my stupid face. "So what do we do first?"

"First, get out of this bed and take a shower, dude." Thomas punches me in the arm. "You reek."

After my shower, I find Thomas out in his driveway, changing the oil in his Harley. I sit on the back steps, watching Thomas work. Do I know about engines? Have I ever worked on cars or bikes? Nothing comes, but it doesn't matter. It just feels good to be outside, warm sun on my face, my arms. It's a relief to have let somebody in at last, somebody who might be able to help me.

"You know, I've got it figured out," Thomas says after a while, sliding a metal pan under the oil tank. He rests on his haunches and looks at me. "I know who you are."

Startled, I turn to stare at him. "You do?"

He stands up and grabs a wrench from a neatly organized tool chest on the driveway. "Yep. I suspected it from the first moment I saw you at the cabin site, looking like you were transported there from some other time or place. Remember?"

"Yeah, I remember."

"And then when you were unconscious, you started talking."

"Really? What did I say?"

"You were quoting entire phrases of Walden, verbatim."

"Which means that—" I have a photographic memory.

"That you're Henry Thoreau reincarnated." Thomas interrupts, pointing his wrench at me triumphantly.

I stare at him, my mouth hanging open.

"I mean, just look at you," he continues. "Dark hair, gray eyes, just like Henry. And you know his writing by heart. I think it's a reasonable explanation, don't you?"

"Reincarnated? Thomas, I don't think—"

Thomas starts to chuckle, and I realize he's just yanking my chain. But then he stops laughing and jabs a finger at me. "*If you have built castles in the air, your work need not be lost—*"

"*That is where they should be. Now put the foundations under them,*" I say without thinking.

Thomas nods to himself. After another moment, he turns to me again. "*I would rather sit on a pumpkin and have it all to myself—*" he says and waits.

"*Than be crowded on a velvet cushion.*"

He stares into my face, eyes intense. "*A lake is the landscape's most beautiful and expressive feature,*" he says.

"*It is earth's eye,*" I respond. "*Looking into which the beholder…*uh…wait, I'll get it." I rack my brain, and nothing comes to me. Could be from one of the pages

Frankie ate. Or maybe my memory isn't as great as I thought. "Nope. No idea what's next."

"That proves nothing. Not even Henry could recite every single word he wrote," Thomas says and shrugs. "I still say you could be him reincarnated. Why not? There are far weirder things in this world, Hank."

I shake my head. "You have a lot of strange ideas, Thomas."

"I know. I get that a lot," he says cheerfully. Gotta admire a guy who's clearly comfortable with his own quirks. "But if anything comes to you about Henry's love life—or lack thereof—let me know. There are a lot of Thoreau scholars who have questions we'd like to get cleared up on the subject."

"Promise."

Thomas smiles at me and winks. Then he turns back to his Harley and loosens the bolt on the oil tank with his wrench, giving the job his full attention like he's already forgotten all about me and his bizarre theory.

Thoreau reincarnated? Ha. If that's true, then I'm totally screwing up Henry's second chance at life. Just one more reason to feel like a loser.

Sitting there on the steps in the sun, watching Thomas change the oil in his motorcycle, my mind wanders to that beautiful butterscotch Tele that Thomas has in the guest room. If I'm really careful, I wonder if he'll let me play it.

And then I'm struck by a scrap of thought. An old memory? No, a new one. There's that thing I forgot to remember. Something I was supposed to do before I got sick. Damn, what was that? Then I remember. Hailey.

I never called Hailey.

The last time we spoke, when I said I'd call her, was days ago. She's going to think I blew her off.

"Thomas, can I borrow your phone?"

Hailey answers her phone on the first ring, and at first I have no idea what to say.

"Uh, Hailey? It's Hank."

No answer.

"Hailey?"

"Yeah, I'm here."

"I'm so sorry I didn't call. I was sick. I mean, seriously, there was this infection, and I was really out of it for a while."

"What do you want, Hank?"

Damn.

"Well, I thought we might get together. You know.

Play some music. Like we said."

She makes me sweat it out and doesn't answer for a good ten seconds, though it feels a lot longer. "Sure," she says at last, like she doesn't really care. "Come over to my house tomorrow at four. I should be back from lacrosse practice by then."

She gives me the address and hangs up kind of abruptly, but I don't care, because she's giving me a chance to redeem myself. Standing in Thomas's front hallway, still holding the phone, I feel a goofy smile spread across my face. I'm going to see Hailey. Tomorrow. *Yes.*

SUZANNE DROPS ME OFF ON THE WAY TO HER AFTERNOON shift at Emerson (as in Ralph Waldo, of course) Hospital, and I show up on Hailey's doorstep, holding Thomas's guitar in one hand and a small amp in the other.

When Hailey answers the door, I notice she's wearing jeans and this tight purple shirt. She looks amazing. We're shy with each other at first, so we don't say much of anything past hi and come on in. She leads the way through a front hallway and I follow, noticing that she's not wearing shoes and her socks are two different colors, which reminds me of her unmatched earrings the other day. Either she has a habit of losing socks and earrings or she's making some kind of quirky fashion statement.

Her house is one of the smaller ones in her neighbor-hood, which basically means it's a normal size. The other houses look way too big for one family, like mansions. Even though it's smaller than the neighbors, it's decorated really nice, with fancy furniture and paintings and Oriental carpets. She leads me into a room that's all white. No kidding. White rug, white sofas, white walls, even a white grand piano. I'm afraid to have a dirty thought in this room. Which is difficult, considering the way I'm starting to feel about Hailey.

"Wow, you could hide a polar bear in this room if you wanted to," I say. Lame, but a smile twitches at the corners of Hailey's mouth, which is good enough for me.

"My mother likes to do dramatic decorating stuff. It's just annoying."

She shows me where I can plug in the amp, then I sit on one of those white sofas and tune up the guitar. Sensing that Hailey is not in the mood for small talk, I let my fingers launch into a random tune, just to warm up and get used to the guitar. It plays real nice. Smooth.

As I'm playing, Hailey finally smiles at me, then shakes her head and bursts out laughing. She has a great laugh.

"Cute," she says.

I stop playing, fingers suspended above the strings. "What?"

"That song you're playing."

I stare at her and blink like a total idiot. "I'm sorry?"

"Come on, Hank. You're kidding me, right? You're playing 'White Room,' by Cream. My mom is a big Eric Clapton fan too."

Clapton. Of course. In my real life, I must be a big-time classic rock geek, and this crazy room triggered my muscle memory. I smile at her like, yeah, "White Room." I meant to do that.

Now that I've got Hailey in a good mood, I start in on the song we played in the band room, "Blackbird." The Beatles. She lets me play the first verse all the way through before she starts singing. Her voice is quiet at first, almost a whisper, but then she clears her throat and allows her voice to rise. Again, that gorgeous, silky alto voice. Funny how just a voice can drive me crazy. I finish the song and we just stare at each other like we're holding our breath waiting for what comes next.

"Hailey," I say. "Your voice just blows me away."

She looks down at her fingernails, picks at some red polish on her thumb, and I figure she's just being shy. But when she looks back up at me, her eyes have gotten all shimmery.

"Thanks, but it doesn't do me any good if I'm too scared to get up and sing."

I stare at her, my eyebrows crunching together in disbelief. "Why would somebody like you ever be scared to sing?"

"Something bad happened. Last year, at the Battle of the Bands."

"What, like stage fright? Hey, that happens to a lot of people."

"No. I wish that's all it was." Hailey clears her throat, avoids my eyes. "Remember the day we met, when Danielle was bugging me about looking kind of sick?"

"Yeah, I do." I'd thought of asking her about that, but figured it might still be a sore subject.

"Well, it's like this. I'm diabetic. My blood sugar was starting to crash after lacrosse practice, so I got a little dizzy. After you left, I had to drink some juice to jolt it back up."

Diabetic. My damaged memory banks seem to recall what that is. Something about the pancreas and insulin. "Is that what happened at the Battle of the Bands too?"

"Yeah, but it was much, much worse. I was nervous, so I didn't eat much that day. Didn't even think about it. By the time I was up on stage, I went into this full-out insulin reaction. I mean, I passed out and started having this seizure, in front of everybody. They had to call an ambulance and everything. It was humiliating."

Tears stand in her eyes, ready to roll down her cheeks. I wish I could magically say the right thing to make it better. "You couldn't help that. I'm sure everybody understood."

"The problem is, almost nobody knew about the diabetes. I've had it since I was about nine, but I don't like to talk about it. Just don't want to be *different*, you know? So everybody kind of freaked out, and some people still seem scared to be around me, in case it happens again."

She wipes at her eyes and tries to smile at me. "Needless to say, I haven't sung in public since then."

I shake my head. "That's so wrong, Hailey. You should do the show this year. Seriously. You have to."

"I don't know, Hank. Maybe—"

The doorbell rings.

"Hang on, I gotta get that," she says. "My parents are still at work."

She leaves the white room and heads to the front door, so I play around some more with the guitar. It feels so natural, fingers on my left hand flying across the frets, fingers on my right strumming and picking. Like I was born to do this. Like when I'm with Hailey and making music, nothing else matters. The ultimate escape, the best drug ever.

I stop playing when I hear voices arguing.

"I don't want to, Cam. Can't you get somebody else?"

I pause with my fingers hovering over the strings and listen. It's Cameron.

"You said you'd do it, Hailey. What else am I supposed to do? Plus, not to be mean or anything, but you owe me."

"God, Cam. How long am I going to owe you?"

I set the guitar down, lean it against the sofa.

"C'mon, Hailey, you know the deal."

I walk to the front door and stand behind Hailey like a bodyguard, arms crossed over my chest, hoping it will make my biceps look more substantial than they actually are. "You okay, Hailey?"

He looks surprised, then pissed to see me there with Hailey, at her house. And in spite of my macho stance, I'm praying this isn't the time he chooses to pick a fight, when I'm still really weak.

"Yeah, I'm okay," Hailey says over her shoulder.

Cameron looks like he wants to take me down, and I'm glad he doesn't know he could knock me over with one finger if he really tried. But then he starts looking me over from head to toe, shrewd eyes sweeping.

"So, Hank, where did you get that shirt?" he demands.

I look down. Long-sleeved black T-shirt, white words. From the high school lost and found. "I dunno," I say.

"Why are you so fascinated by my wardrobe, Cam?"

"Because my dad got me a shirt just like it from the Nashville Music Hall of Fame. That's what it says on the front. I lost that shirt about a week ago. The same time you just happened to appear out of nowhere. Not a shirt you see every day in Concord, Massachusetts, don't you think?"

Uh-oh.

Hailey rolls her eyes. "So what are you saying, Cam? That Hank stole your shirt?"

"I'm just saying it's a really weird coincidence."

"The world is full of really weird coincidences," I say.

"Look, Cam, I think you should go," Hailey says. "We'll talk about that other thing later."

Cameron glares at both of us, and I almost laugh out loud. He's trying to look all tough and badass with his scuffed-up black boots and sideways cap. I fight the urge to smack the hat right off his head.

"Yeah, we'll talk about a lot of things later," he says. He jabs a finger in the air as he turns and heads back down the front brick steps. "And I want my shirt back, douchebag," he says.

Hailey closes the door and leans back against it, biting her lip. "Sorry about that," she says. "Things with Cam and me. They're kinda complicated."

"Yeah, I get that."

She looks like she wants to tell me more, but she shakes her head, pastes on a smile for me. "Forget Cam. Let's make music, Hank."

The magic words. And so we do. We play "Blackbird," and then I mess around with a few more songs my fingers seem to know by heart, and she joins in where she knows the words. Music creates a bond between us, an intimacy. Like touching her with music instead of fingers.

Her red hair and that purple shirt against the white sofa are like a painting or a photograph, like the white room was created just so she could stand out in contrast, in beautiful, amazing color. We finish another song. Taking a break from the music is like coming out of a trance and we can't seem to break free from the way our eyes are locked together.

If ever there was a time for kissing a girl, this is it. But I hesitate. I have no right to kiss Hailey, to get close to her or let her get close to me. My life is just one huge question mark and it wouldn't be fair.

I tear my eyes away from her. Time to change the subject, catch my breath, diffuse the moment. "So, Hailey. What's with the socks and earrings? You have something against things that match?"

Hailey sticks out her feet and wiggles her toes. "They match," she insists.

"They do not. Look, one sock has black cats, the other one has blue...what are those?" I lean in for a closer look. "Elephants?"

"Hippos. Both socks have animals; therefore, they match."

I raise an eyebrow. "It's about a theme, then?" I ask, like we're having a super-serious discussion.

"Yeah, like I might wear a green striped sock with a pink striped one. Both stripes. Or a star earring in one ear, a moon in the other. Got it?"

"Hmm. So, it's not just that you're too lazy to find the ones that go together?"

"Well, okay, it started like that," she admits, finally cracking a smile. "But, of course, I told everybody I did it on purpose, and it sort of got to be my trademark. It's not easy to get away with being a nonconformist in Concord, so I do what I can."

We smile into each other's eyes, and there's that thing again, and I'm not even sure what to call it. Magnetism, maybe. Chemistry. Magic.

"I like it," I say, meaning it. "Symmetry is overrated anyway."

I want to kiss her, so bad. But I don't make a move. I can't. So finally, Hailey does.

Kneeling in front of me without a word, she removes the guitar from my hands and leans it against the couch, and I let her do it. Then she puts her hands on both sides of my face. Her lips are soft and sweet, like cherry candy. I get lost completely in that kiss, the same way I got lost in our music.

"So we're doing this thing, right?" Her breath is warm in my ear and makes me shiver. With where my mind is heading, I'm taken totally off guard by the question.

"Uh. Doing what?"

"The Battle of the Bands. After we sang together in the band room that day, I actually started thinking I might be able to do it if you'll help me. Will you, Hank?"

So. Hang on a second. Only a few days ago I realized I can play guitar, and I'm already going to perform in public? Am I crazy out of my mind?

Well. Yeah, I am. For Hailey, I am.

I nod, and she makes this happy squealy sound. Then she kisses me again.

No matter what I've done or who I am, it's clear that this funny, talented, pretty girl really likes me. So maybe, just maybe, when it comes right down to it, I'm not such a bad person after all.

11

"HERE YOU GO. I FOUND A COUPLE MORE." THOMAS BRINGS over two more books and sets them on top of the stack he already gave me. Jesus. The guy is just way too into this research thing.

Sitting in the Thoreau room at the library, I flip through books on memory and memory loss, hopefully to get a handle on how this thing happened to me and, maybe, how to reverse it. I'm not sure the answer to that lies in these books, but Thomas is all about research, so whatever.

Amnesia can be caused by physical trauma like a crack on the head, the books say. Or, it can be a result of emotional trauma. Like if something really terrible happened, too traumatic to deal with, your brain blocks it out. It's the brain protecting itself, a defense mechanism. Kind of cool and weird at the same time, when you think about it.

Basically all the books agree on one thing: the brain is a mystery. And what causes memory loss and what brings it back are things people don't completely understand. Great. That's no help at all.

What if I never get my memory back? I figure I have two choices: Create a life with no past, starting here and now. Or go to the Concord Police Department and turn myself in. They'd call the media and put me on the news, and eventually someone would see me and identify me. I'd be taken home to parents I don't remember, a life that I apparently ran away from. If they want me back, that is. Then there's the chance that I'm facing jail time. All of which make option number one sound like the best choice: creating my own life, on my own terms, something like what Thoreau did.

"Did those books help?" Thomas asks me, setting one more book on top of the pile, which threatens to topple over.

"Basically they say I might remember a little at a time, remember everything at once, or never remember another thing for the rest of my life."

"Hmm," says Thomas, scratching his bearded chin. "Well, that leaves things pretty much open, doesn't it?"

162

"Yeah," I say, leaning back with my feet straight out and my arms crossed over my chest, shutting down. "Sucks."

"Listen, Hank, I have an idea. There's this database for missing kids. We can bring it up on the computer and see if you're on it."

He signs me up for one of the library computers, and together we go online. And there it is, the National Center for Missing and Exploited Children. My heart jumps in my chest, just looking at those words. Missing. Exploited. Which am I?

"Any particular state you'd like to start with?" Thomas asks.

"How about New York," I say. Makes sense. It's where I woke up.

A few swipes on the keyboard, and he has opened up a page of missing kids from the state of New York. Over a hundred of them.

"Okay, Hank, go to it," Thomas says. "I need to get back to work. Let me know if you find anything significant."

"You're brilliant," I tell him.

"I know. Although, of course, if you don't find yourself listed there, it's just one more bit of evidence to prove my little theory."

"That I'm the second coming of Thoreau," I say dryly.

"Exactly." He heads back toward his desk, then stops and says quickly, *"If a man loses pace with his companions—"*

"Perhaps it is because he hears a different drummer. Let him step to the music which he hears, however measured, or far away. Oh come on, Thomas. That was an easy one."

Leaning over the computer screen with sweaty palms, I scan the pictures and read the listings. Date of birth. Age. Date the kid went missing. There are endangered runaways. Endangered missing. Family abduction. Non-family abduction. A John Doe with no picture is a possible homicide victim. This is a scary world to be visiting, even online, and somehow I'm a part of it. Creepy.

I'm confused when I see pictures of adults, with ages like forty-five or fifty-seven, until I realize they've been missing since they were kids. Somebody did age-progression computer imaging and some of the people look weirdly unnatural. I guess it's not easy to take a picture of a four-year-old and try to figure out what he or she would look like at age fifty-seven. God, there are families who never give up, ever. Is my family one of those? Or were they glad when I disappeared? *Nobody will miss you.*

I check all the pictures of the missing children from New York, and I don't find myself there. So I decide there's nothing to do but start from the beginning with Alabama and go through every single state in the country, look at every single picture of every single missing kid, to see if I pop up.

Two hours later, my back is cramping up, I've only made it as far as Connecticut, and all the faces are starting to look the same. What a depressing task this is. All these kids with families who can't find them. Or even worse, all the John Does and Jane Does who have been found, probably dead, and nobody even knows who they are, or were.

If I were to turn myself in to the police, is that what they'd call me? John Doe? A chill prickles down my spine.

That chill climbs up my neck and into the roots of my hair when I look at the last page of pictures from Connecticut. That's when I see a face I know and almost fall right out of my chair. The kid's hair is combed and cut shorter and the clothes are actually clean, but I still know him. I know the straight nose, the strong mouth and that stubborn tilt of his chin, like he's daring someone to smash him in the jaw.

Jack.

John Alexander Zane, the listing says. Endangered runaway. His date of birth tells me he turned sixteen last week. He has been missing from Bridgeport, Connecticut, for about a month. So he and Nessa had only been on the streets for a month?

One picture beneath his is the female version of Jack. It's Nessa, smiling in what looks like a high school portrait. I hadn't realized how much they look alike. Vanessa Lee Zane. She's barely fifteen.

For a second, I want to call the number listed and report that I've seen them, so at least one of these desperate families can know what happened to their kids. Maybe there's an aunt or somebody who would take them in, get them away from Magpie and off the streets. But then I remember the look on Jack's face when he said he'd never go back home. Something bad happened with their dad, and I can't be the one to potentially send them back to it.

Thomas pops in to check on me. "Anything yet?" I decide not to tell him about Jack and Nessa, figuring it would do nobody any good.

I shrug. "Not yet. My neck is starting to cramp up from all this computer stuff."

"So close it down for now and come help me," Thomas says. "We've got a bunch of shelving to do over in fiction. I could slip you a few bucks if you'll help me out. Sound good?"

I grin at him. "Money always sounds good."

The Battle of the Bands is only one week away, but Hailey is able to pull together a couple musicians to play with us. The drummer is this laid-back stocky guy named Sam who plays in the school jazz band, and the bass player is a friend of hers from English lit class, named Ryan. Ryan, a short, thin guy with glasses, has never played with a band before, but she says he's taking lessons and is ready to play. So we all show up together to rehearse for the first time Monday afternoon on the high school stage. Hailey introduces me to everybody as a new transfer student. I wonder how long I'll be able to get away with that.

Secrecy, as it turns out, is a big part of the Battle of the Bands event at Thoreau High. The windows on the auditorium doors are covered with black paper so nobody can peek in from the hallway, and only one band at a time rehearses with the stage crew to keep everything a surprise until performance night.

Bands are allowed to play one to three songs. Of course we choose just one, "Blackbird," hoping we can even pull *that* off. Sam, Ryan, Hailey, and I set up our gear on the stage and take a few moments to tune up.

"Okay, let's try it like this," I suggest. "It'll start with Hailey and me, guitar and voice, for the first part of the song, nice and easy like a ballad. But as we go into it a second time, you guys join in and we totally rock it out through the end. Want to give it a shot?"

We start the song just like Hailey and I had been practicing in the white room. Guitar and voice, the two of us together. Hailey starts out strong, with that gorgeous voice of hers. But then, she starts to waver.

She stops singing, swallows hard. "Can we start over?" she asks me.

"Of course."

"Need something, Hailey?" Ms. Coleman asks from the auditorium seats. "I brought a few candy bars along just in case."

Hailey looks embarrassed but shakes her head. "No, I'm fine," she says. "Just nerves."

I begin the intro again, cutting her a meaningful look. *You can do this, Hailey.*

Even though her voice is tentative, she makes it through the song the first time through, and the rest of the band comes crashing in. It's total chaos. We sound like crap.

"Whoa. Hold on, hold on," I say, waving my arms to

stop them. "You came in too soon. And Ryan, you have that progression wrong. I don't know what that last note was, but it wasn't right."

Ryan's face turns bright red, but he nods. "You're right," he says. "Sorry, just a little nervous. I'll get it."

I take a deep breath and remind myself this was our first time through. Not a total disaster, not yet. Relax. "Let's start from where you guys come in, okay?" I count it off, and we sail into the next verse. Sam gets it immediately, adding just the right touches on snare and cymbal. Ryan screws up again, but at least we finish the verse.

"I'll get it," Ryan insists.

We take it from the top again, and this time, Hailey sounds stronger. We limp through the part with Ryan, then do it again. And again.

"Okay, it's almost time for the next group to come in." Ms. Coleman comes up and joins us on the stage. "That's… really coming along." Which is probably the nicest thing she can think of to say. "So let's talk staging and some really basic special effects. What did you have in mind?"

I shrug. All my focus was just on the music, but clearly Hailey has been thinking about the rest. She and Ms. Coleman sit on the edge of the stage, and Ms. Coleman makes notes on a yellow legal pad.

"Sounds great, Sam," I tell the drummer. "Ryan, well, dude, you're getting there."

Ryan's face burns as he puts his bass in its case. "I'll work on it at home. I'll get it," he says again.

"I know you will," I say, hoping like hell.

"One more thing," Ms. Coleman says. "What's the name of your band?"

The four of us look at each other. We hadn't given that detail any thought at all.

"Can we get back to you on that?" Hailey asks.

"All right, just let me know as soon as possible so we can put it in the program," says Ms. Coleman. "Good work today. Be here at seven on Saturday, ready to play."

"We will," Hailey says. She turns to the rest of us. "Can you all practice at my house Wednesday afternoon? Like three o'clock?" Everybody says yes.

Her cheeks are pink and she looks excited, but there's this wild thing lurking behind her green eyes and I know she's also terrified that this year will be a replay of what happened last time. I want to tell her to relax, it's going to be great, that she's going to be amazing.

But I never get the chance, because just then the back door of the auditorium crashes shut like a gunshot. This time, thank God, I don't collapse onto the floor. But then I see who came in, letting the door slam like he did it on purpose: Cameron. And he looks pissed.

"Uh-oh," I hear Hailey breathe beside me.

"Cameron, you know the rules," says Ms. Coleman. "You're supposed to wait in the hall until someone from the crew comes to get you."

Cameron's eyes are locked onto Hailey's, but he responds to Ms. Coleman. "I'm sorry. Guess I forgot."

"That's okay, I think these folks are done." She shoots Hailey a questioning glance, and Hailey nods. "You can bring your group in now, Cameron."

"Cameron has a group?" I whisper to Hailey.

"Yep," she says, biting her lip. "It used to be my group."

While Sam, Ryan, and I gather our gear together, Cameron pulls Hailey over to the side of the stage and I try to eavesdrop. They talk in hushed tones so it's hard to hear, until the voices rise in argument. Coiling a cable, I draw closer to listen.

"Why the hell should you care? You have another lead singer now," Hailey says.

"That's only because you said you wouldn't do it," Cameron argues, yanking his cap off, as if his anger makes it too tight on his head. Their voices lower again and I can't hear the rest.

"Hank."

Someone calls my name from the auditorium doorway. Sophie the janitor stands in the hallway, waving me over with a blue rag in her hand. What does she want? Am I in trouble? Did she or the dread-lock janitor decide to turn me in? Pushing aside my nervousness, I hop off the stage to join her.

"Hey, Sophie," I say, all casual. "What's up?"

Sophie's kind brown eyes scan my face like she's trying to absorb that part of me that reminds her of her son.

"Did your friends ever find you?" she asks. Her gray-black hair is wild today, full of static electricity. Like if I touch it, I might get a shock.

"What friends?"

"They came into the school asking after some new kid, and from their description, I knew immediately it was you." She wipes her hands on the blue cloth and stuffs it into the back pocket of her overalls.

Ice-cold fear trumps the nervousness in my gut. "What did these people look like, Sophie?" I fight an urge to shake her.

"They were two young men, like you," she says. "But of course, most people look young to me these days." Her smile creates a web of wrinkles around her eyes, but my face is frozen and I can't smile back.

Could she mean Magpie? Was it naïve of me to think

Magpie would just give up and let me go? After all, we know too much about each other. I know he's into drug dealing and taking advantage of street kids, and he knows what I did to Simon in that alley. But it's not possible that he tracked me all the way to Concord. Is it?

"Are you doing okay, Hank?" Sophie looks like she wants to check me again for signs of a fever. "Ever since you left the school, I've been worried about you."

"Oh, sure," I say, forcing a smile. "I'm fine, really." She's a sweet lady, but I just want to be done talking to her. In fact, I want to bolt out of this room. "Thanks for letting me know about my, uh, friends."

The auditorium door slams shut again, jarring me to the bone, and there's a flurry of voices as the rest of Cameron's band files into the room, pulling Cameron away from Hailey to set up. The lead singer is this skinny girl dressed all in black with straight blond hair, dyed pink at the tips. She gives Hailey a superior smirk, like she's proud that she's taken Hailey's place in the band. Whatever. There's no way she's as good.

Ms. Coleman shoos us out of the auditorium so Cameron's band can set up. Out in the hallway, we say good-bye to Sam and Ryan and they take off, leaving Hailey and me alone together. Her cheeks are red after her exchange with Cameron, and her green eyes flash.

"Let's get out of here," I suggest. "You want to go downtown?"

"Yes. Need ice cream, stat," she says and manages a tight smile. "By the way, what did the janitor want? I saw her talking to you."

"Nothing. She just kind of likes me, I guess."

"Of course she does." Hailey reaches over, so easy, and takes my hand. Hers is warm and soft and fits perfectly into mine. "She's a sweet lady, but a little crazy," she says with a shrug. "That's what people say anyway."

"Yeah." But I know she's not that crazy. Still, it's not possible that somebody really did come looking for me, not here in Concord, Massachusetts. Is it?

Don't think about it.

12

Helen's Restaurant is packed with the after-school crowd. A hum of laughter and conversation floats in the small space like smoke, punctuated by scraping forks on plates, the clink of soda glasses behind the breakfast counter. We sit in a booth across from each other, and Hailey orders a strawberry sundae with extra whipped cream. I'm not hungry, so I just get a root beer.

"Don't judge me," she says, her spoon poised above the sundae.

"Why would I do that?"

"Danielle is always lecturing me about what I eat. Drives me crazy."

"I wouldn't judge you," I tell her, wondering what ice cream has to do her health, making a mental note to find out. "Anyway, tell me about Cameron," I say, glad I have something to take my mind off what Sophie said.

Hailey licks a few drips off her spoon. "It's kind of a long story."

I tie a double knot in the paper left over from my straw and smile at her. "I've got time."

So she tells me about how her parents and Cameron's parents have been best friends and next-door neighbors since the two of them were in kindergarten. They grew up like cousins, with both families really close. His family helped them through the scary time when Hailey got sick, before they knew what was wrong. Then they started a band freshman year, with Cameron on lead guitar and Hailey on vocals. The band fell apart after last year's doomed—her word—Battle of the Bands, but the two of them were still close friends. This past fall, they decided to try dating. It didn't take.

"I don't know. He started getting serious right away, you know? But I realized it wasn't like that for me. He's more like a brother than a boyfriend. So I broke it off. And he was really crushed. Things haven't been the same between us since."

Hailey hands me an extra spoon. I take a bite of her sundae, sweet cold strawberry, and although it's good, I realize hot fudge would have been my choice. Another new detail I know about myself.

"And what was that thing he wants you to do for him, the thing you owe him, or whatever?" I ask, setting the spoon back on the table.

Her mouth twists to one side and she frowns. "Yeah, well, here's the thing. A couple weeks ago, I went to this party and had way too much to drink. It's not something I do very often because it's really bad for me, but I was stupid. Had a sucky day or whatever. Anyway, I was even more stupid to try and drive myself home. I was in my own neighborhood when I took a turn too sharp, and smashed right into a tree at the end of my street. I was totally freaking out. So I went hammering on Cam's door because I didn't know what else to do. His parents and mine were out together at a play in the city. So he came out and saw the car. One of our neighbors had called the police, and we knew they were on their way.

"He said to tell them he was driving, but I said no, I couldn't do that, because then he'd get in trouble. 'Not as much as you,' he said. And he was right. So I did it. I let him get in the car, in the driver's seat. And when the police came, he said he'd swerved to avoid hitting a dog. The police totally bought it. But the thing is, he has a junior license, he's not supposed to have a passenger in the car, that's one of the rules. So his license is suspended for sixty days."

"Well the license thing, that's not your fault," I say, hating that Cameron has any excuse to manipulate her. The waitress comes by and gives me a refill on my root beer, without me even having to ask.

"No, but it still comes down to this: he did me a huge favor and kept me from getting a DUI on my license, and probably having to pay a huge fine and go to driving classes. So I do owe him. To a point anyway." Hailey's spoon clinks against glass as she scoops up the last few spoonfuls of melted ice cream.

"I don't know. It sounds like he's totally taking advantage of the situation."

"No doubt about that. Anyway, let's not talk about this anymore." With a flourish, she takes the last bite of her sundae and then licks her lips. She has no idea what this does to me. Or maybe she does and just wants to torture me a little. I fight the urge to grab her, right here in this booth, and kiss the last traces of whipped cream off her lips.

"Come on, I'll give you a ride back to your uncle's house," she says.

"My uncle?"

"Yeah. Didn't you say that's where you're staying?" She looks at me for a minute like I'm a bug under a microscope. "Seriously, sometimes I feel like I don't know anything about you, Hank. Mr. Mysterious. Who the hell are you anyway?"

"I have no idea," I say, flashing a charming smile to show her I'm kidding. "It's just that, uh, he's more like a friend of the family than an actual relative. I just call him uncle. Uncle Thomas."

"Is he your teacher, then?"

"What do you mean?"

"For homeschooling. Does he teach you?"

"Oh." I clear my throat, shuffle my feet under the table. "No, I do it myself. On the computer and stuff. That's how it works." God, I hope that's how it works.

She squints at me, but then shrugs, like she's accepted my explanation. Whew.

"By the way, I told Ms. Coleman your situation, with the homeschooling and all, to make sure it's okay for you to be in the Battle of the Bands. I didn't want them kicking you out at the last minute or anything."

My stomach drops. "And?"

"And she said it was okay. She's cool like that. Plus, she really likes you."

Whew, again. "Good."

To celebrate these small victories and also because I can't hold back any longer, I kiss her. And she tastes delicious, like strawberries and whipped cream and Hailey.

Letting myself get lost in the moment, the knot in my gut relaxes. Hailey makes me feel like I'm worth something and that I'm safe here. Surely here in this good place with this amazing girl, nothing bad could happen and nobody could hurt me. Not even Magpie. I want to believe this, so bad. And so for the moment, I do.

Riding on the back of Thomas's motorcycle on the way to the library the next morning, there's this comfortable hum in my chest. The air is getting warmer and smells like black dirt and new grass. I have a great place to stay with Thomas. I'm making music with Hailey and falling for her more every day. Concord is a nice town, and with the exception maybe of Cameron, it's full of really nice people. It occurs to me I haven't felt the beast attack my insides for days. Not since waking up at Thomas's place last week. To me, that's huge.

Thoreau wrote that we should suck the marrow out of life. Okay, so this may not be the life I started with. But it's a good one at the moment, so why not go ahead and seize the day?

For about an hour, I hum to myself, re-shelving books in the nonfiction stacks at the library. But then I have to bring a cart of books into the Thoreau room and I stop short outside the room, where the head and shoulders statue of Henry David sits on a pedestal. My heart sinks in my chest.

Thoreau's statue-blank eyes aren't saying anything to me about sucking the marrow out of life or seizing the day. What they're saying instead, is: *what the hell are you doing, Hank, allowing yourself to settle into a life where you don't belong? Have you gotten so unbelievably selfish that you've forgotten all about your sister?*

Trying to ignore a sick feeling spreading in the pit of my stomach, I finish up the shelving and then sit my butt back down at the library computer. I don't want to look through the Missing and Exploited Children database anymore, and I hate that I can't live a normal, everyday life and just be happy. But I have no choice. I have to keep searching for the truth. Not for my sake anymore, but my sister's. And if someone has come to Concord looking for me, I might not have a lot of time.

Picking up where I left off, I look at every single kid in the database who vanished from Delaware. Then Florida, Georgia, Hawaii. So many faces, so many missing kids, so many broken families. The faces all seem to blur together. But I continue, on to Idaho. Then Illinois.

Illinois.

That's when it happens. That's when I see the face. My face.

It's me, but somehow it's not me. Same face, same hair, but I'm smiling, confident. A high school picture. High school kid who looks secure in his existence. A guy who seems to know exactly who he is. Or was. A guy named Daniel Henderson. My heart seizes up in my chest.

Daniel Henderson. I say the name to myself, whispering it out loud in the library.

Daniel Henderson, the listing says. From Naperville, Illinois.

So this is me. My real name. I think back to the image I had of my dad, calling my name in Walden Woods. The name I couldn't quite hear him calling was Danny. Yes, that sounds right. I am Danny Henderson from Naperville, Illinois. It says my birth date is May 12, which means I'll turn eighteen in just a few weeks. I must be a senior in high school. Will I miss my own graduation? Was I going to college?

I hold on to the edge of the table, not breathing. Bracing myself, I wait for all of Danny Henderson's memories to come rushing back into me, filling every empty space inside with life and memory and realization.

But nothing comes. I can't believe it. Nothing comes.

I'm not Hank, but Danny. So why do I still feel like Hank?

I look over at Thomas, where he sits at his desk, entering information into his computer. I'm not ready to tell Thomas. I need to take time with this, need to get a grip. Where the hell is Naperville, Illinois? Will I remember, if I research the town where Danny Henderson lived?

I take a break, wander around the room, and stretch my legs. My heart is pounding against my ribs like I'm going to have a coronary. Can't take too much of this all at once. Can't seem to absorb it. I go down to the candy machine. Buy M&Ms. Make myself eat them slowly, one at a time, by color. Red, blue, yellow, green. Then I return to the computer and sit down.

Search: *Naperville, Illinois.*

There's a website for the town. I look at pictures of the downtown area. There's a riverwalk. It's a big town with four high schools, one of them mine. But which one? Pretty houses in the suburbs, sort of like Concord. Danny Henderson lived in this nice suburban town, about forty minutes west of Chicago. Maybe I rooted for the Bulls. The Bears. The White Sox or the Cubs? My gut says Cubs, but I can't be sure.

There's a link on the website to the local newspaper

called the *Naperville Sun*. I take my disappearance date, April 10, which is listed on the Missing and Exploited Children site and I search the archives of the Naperville Sun for a couple days before my disappearance. There are articles about local politicians, church suppers, and ads about local stores having sales. Nothing seems familiar.

That's when I see the headline on the sports page, and a dim lightbulb of memory switches on somewhere in a dark back hallway of my brain.

NAPERVILLE SOUTH BOYS TRACK TEAM FACES RIVALS

The track team is posed in one of those yearbook-type pictures with the guys standing in two rows, wearing team uniforms with numbers. The taller guys are in the back. I scan their faces and stop. One of them is me. Not smiling, just standing there like I want the photographer to take the picture already so I can leave. And then there, right under the team picture is another photo, an action shot featuring some dark-haired guy with arms pumping, legs flying like something's chasing him. His face is a grimace, eyes wide, mouth open like he's sucking air. The guy is me.

Senior Daniel Henderson trains for spring track season at Naperville South. Henderson excelled last year and is expected to challenge or break long-standing school records this season. The Naperville South runners will face off against their rivals from Aurora West this Saturday at home.

With detached curiosity I stare at this Daniel Henderson, huffing and puffing his way through a race, examine the contorted face of a stranger. I feel nothing.

But then slowly, a sensation creeps up on me, like a ripple circling from a stone thrown in a pond. It grows into a wave, starting somewhere in the roots of my hair, reaching tendrils into my scalp and neck and face, and I feel the flush, a red burn spreading over every surface of my skin. And then, with a deep shudder to the bone, to the brain, to the heart, I switch places and I become that boy.

Cold April air rushes down my throat, prickles my lungs. Arms and legs pump like pistons and I'm a machine, oblivious to everything but my muscles on fire, my body propelling itself through space, weaving past the other runners, toward the finish line.

Except that in truth, I'm not running around the high school track in Naperville, Illinois, at all. I'm bolting for the library door. Sprinting past Thomas, who looks up in surprise.

His voice, too loud for the library, is like sounding an alarm: "Hank, what's wrong?!"

I almost fall down the concrete steps, vision bombarded with black-red flashes as the beast roars to life from its pit inside me. But it's not just one beast, not anymore. It divides itself into a billion smaller versions of itself, each with curled claws, red eyes, rising, choking, leaping at my throat, trying to kill me for starting to remember what is crucial to forget.

Down the sidewalk, toward town. Feet pounding on pavement. Left on Thoreau Street, right on Walden. Cross Route Two. Arms pumping, keep moving. Running until I reach Walden Pond. Running along the path that rings the pond, then branching off and bolting into the woods. Crashing through the underbrush. Still running, sweat streams down my face into my mouth, salty. Past the railroad tracks, deeper into the woods. Trying to outrun the snarling beasts, desperate to find the calm that comes with running.

And somehow I find a way to outrun the terror by forcing myself back in time, before the memory of lights swirling red and blue, before the pink ballerina broken, before the blood.

Settling my body into the cadence of running, the steady inhale, exhale pattern that keeps my heart from beating out of control, I begin to remember my life.

The last good day was cold for early April. My breath came in white clouds as I went for my morning run around the neighborhood, nothing too long or crazy, just a chance to stretch my legs and wake up my brain. When I got home, I wheeled the green trash barrel to the curb, like I did every Friday morning of my life. The sky was milky and the air smelled like snow, but I was sure it wouldn't dare snow, not this weekend. The next day was the big meet against Aurora. That night, I had plans.

The recycle bins went next, overflowing with empty cereal boxes, newspapers, and soup cans. Every week, I counted the empty wine bottles. More than three meant that Mom had a bad week.

After I showered and got dressed for school, I came downstairs and found my mother standing at the kitchen stove, cooking us cheesy scrambled eggs and bacon. I remember the bacon crackling in the pan, how it smelled, how Mom looked at me with her eyes all soft, and the warmth of the kitchen. I remember home.

"Okay, Danny, here's the info," she said, pointing to a sheet of paper stuck to the fridge with magnets. "This is the hotel where we'll be and here's Aunt June's number in Evanston. Call her if you need help anytime with anything." She turned to me like she still saw a five-year-old standing there. Never mind that I was going to turn eighteen in a month and was six inches taller than her.

"Mom, we're going to be fine," I said. "It's just one weekend, and it's only Galena."

"I know, but it just feels strange to leave the two of you alone," she said, running fingers through her wavy blond hair like she did when she was nervous, which was basically most of the time.

The main reason they wanted to go to Galena this particular weekend was because they got engaged there, exactly twenty years ago. They were obviously trying to bring some magic back to their marriage. I wished them luck on that. Seriously.

"Relax, Mom," Rosie called from the family room, where she was practicing leaps across the carpet in her pink sneakers. "You'll give yourself a myocardial infarction."

Rosie. My sister. Age nine, crazy smart, always dressed in pink. She had this weird habit of throwing big words into normal conversations.

"I think she means a heart attack," Mom said to me. "She must be up to *M* in the World Book."

Rosie loved reading an old set of white-and-green bound encyclopedias my parents had, and spouting off the facts she learned. She had an amazing memory. We both did. Not quite photographic memories—my mom had us tested once—but pretty close.

Dad came down the stairs then, holding that black suitcase he took on business trips. My dad was in sales for a big pharmaceutical company. That's pretty much all I knew about his job. He didn't talk about it. I didn't ask.

"Morning, Rosie Posey," he said, giving my sister a kiss on the cheek. "You going to cheer your brother on at the meet tomorrow, loud enough for all three of us?"

"Of course," she said.

Mom placed plates of cheesy eggs, toast, and bacon on the table, and we all sat down to eat breakfast.

"Oh, by the way, " I said through a mouthful of toast, like something had just occurred to me. Actually, I'd hoped to catch them in a distracted, generous frame of mind before their trip. "There's this thing Joey told me about last night, and I'm thinking of going." Joey was the drummer in my band.

Mom took a sip of coffee. "What kind of thing? When?"

"It's tonight. A concert, actually. And it could be a really great opportunity for, you know, the band."

"Tonight?" Dad asked.

I cleared my throat. "Yeah, see, there's this band coming to the House of Blues, and Joey got tickets through his Uncle Phil, who works there. I told you about him, remember?"

Mom and Dad looked at me blankly. Okay, so I never actually told them about Joey's Uncle Phil, who worked security at the House of Blues in Chicago, but they wouldn't remember that.

"He promised we could get backstage after the show to meet the band. And the lead singer is this guy who runs his own recording label, and he's always looking for fresh talent. And we have that CD we recorded in Matt's basement last month."

"It's really good," Rosie set down her glass and wiped off a milk mustache with the back of her hand. "Best band I ever heard."

Mom glanced over at Dad. He took his time crunching into a burnt slice of bacon.

"Danny, I don't think…"

"Do you realize what an amazing opportunity this is?" I blurted. "I mean, this could be big for the band. Huge. It could be—"

"Your big break?"

"Well. Yeah."

"First of all," Dad said, "you have that big competition tomorrow with a lot riding on it, so you need a good night's sleep. Second, we need you here to watch Rosie. You have family responsibilities, son."

His gray eyes were fixed on me, and I searched them for the good-guy friend version of my dad, the one who took me on camping trips and to Cubs games and shot hoops with me in the driveway on Sunday afternoons. But good-guy Dad had left the building.

"Matt already asked Jessica if she could baby-sit, and she said yes," I said. Matt played bass and sang lead in the band, and his girlfriend thinks Rosie is the cutest kid on the planet. "It'll just be in Chicago so it's no big deal. Joey's uncle will be there. The meet isn't until late afternoon tomorrow, so I'll have plenty of time to rest up."

Dad avoided my eyes. "I'm sorry, Danny," he said. "The meet is just too important to take that chance. The whole team is counting on you."

Figured he'd pull that "whole team counting on you" thing. Like my life wasn't my own. Like the purpose of my existence was to fulfill the expectations of other people. And usually, that's exactly what I did.

Well, almost. There was still that one huge secret I was hiding from Mom and Dad. I never did get around to telling them, not after everything that happened.

"But—"

"End of discussion." Mom got up, gathering plates and silverware, clattering them in the sink like punctuation. Period. Exclamation point.

After they kissed us good-bye and reminded us to do our homework and lock up the house at night, they left for their trip and Rosie and I went out into the garage. Mom was letting me drive her Toyota for the weekend, and I needed to drop Rosie off at school before I went to Naperville South.

Rosie peered out the window and grew silent, which was unusual for her. Usually she gabbed away about school and her friends and the solo she was working on for dance class. And maybe this sounds cheesy as hell, but I listened to her too.

"You okay?" I finally asked her. "You're not worried about Mom and Dad, are you?"

"Nah." She loosened the light blue scarf around her chin. "Not more than usual anyway."

Sometimes she sounded more like a sixteen-year-old than a kid who was nine. It made me a little sad, like she was growing up too fast. "I know what you mean."

When I stopped the car at the curb in front of the school, Rosie just sat there, face nestled into her pink parka, not getting out.

"I want you to go to that concert tonight," she said at last, turning to look at me.

"What?"

"I want you to go to that Blues House place. I like your band. And I really like Jessica too." Her face was solemn, determined. "And I won't tell."

I guess it's pretty clear that Rosie and I were not your typical seventeen-year-old guy and his bratty nine-year-old sister. We'd been through a lot together and were the only people in the world who really understood what it was like to be inside our screwed-up family.

"You mean it?"

"I mean it."

Rosie gave me this huge smile as she grabbed her backpack from the floor, got out of the car, and twirled around once, twice, three times on the grass, before skipping up the front steps to school.

As it turns out, the guys and I never did get to meet the band backstage at the House of Blues that night. I have a vague memory of the concert itself—a headbanger of the first degree—but Joey's stupid Uncle Phil was full of shit.

"I never promised I could get you backstage," Uncle Phil told us after the concert, standing at the stage door with his arms crossed like he was made of stone. "All I said was that I could try and deliver your CD if you wanted."

"That's not what you said yesterday," Joey shot back. "Are you serious, Uncle Phil? Man, I should've just listened to Mom."

"Why? What's she saying about me now?"

"Forget about it." Matt grabbed Joey's shirtsleeve. "Let's just go." He nodded politely at Joey's Uncle Phil. "Thanks for getting us the tickets. It was a great show."

When a defeated Joey handed Phil our CD, I was embarrassed by how amateurish our cover art looked— some guitar in flames that Joey's sister painted for us in art class. But whatever, our sound was good, and that's all that mattered. Phil accepted the CD and nodded at us, purposely avoiding Joey's blazing expression.

"I'll make sure this gets to the right people," he promised us, like he was this amazingly generous guy instead of a total douchebag.

Matt thanked him profusely, I managed a noncommittal shrug, then we all turned and walked in silence to my mom's car. We got in and started the drive back to Naperville.

The thing that happened with the car, now that was just stupid. I'm not sure who was to blame, but it was probably all our faults because we were being loud, yelling stuff out the windows. We weren't hurting anybody, just letting off steam like guys do. Sure, they were drinking rum or whatever Joey stole from his parents' liquor cabinet and put in his dad's flask. He made us laugh all night because he kept taking sneaky sips from it, like a sketchy 1920s guy during Prohibition. Not that I'm a saint or anything, but I wasn't drinking that night. Not just because I was driving, but because I was driving my mom's car. The guys weren't really drunk, just buzzed, but in Joey's case it made him even more obnoxious than usual, which was saying a lot.

"We should just turn around and start pounding on that backstage door until they have to let us in." He grabbed my shoulders from the backseat and shook me. "C'mon, Danny, let's go back and demand they let us talk to the band. I know how to handle my loser Uncle Phil."

"Quit it, Joey, I'm trying to drive." I pushed his hands away.

Matt reached back to smack Joey on the back of the head, and Joey smacked him back, like some Three Stooges routine. I watched in the rearview mirror, laughing and not watching where I was going.

In my defense, there's no way I could've anticipated there would be a huge snowbank at the side of the exit ramp, right where the road curved. No way I could've realized that if a car veered ever so slightly off its correct path because the driver was distracted, it could go plowing right into that freaky April snowbank, parts of which were solid ice after melting and freezing, and cause a scraping sound on the undercarriage of the car that was a sickening combination of crunching snow and metal.

"Ahhh, shit." The car jerked to a stop and a stunned silence settled over the three of us. After a few paralyzed moments of *okay, now what do we do*, we all scrambled out to stare at the car. Fortunately, it was safely off the road and had no visible damage. Unfortunately, it looked like the car was stuck. Really stuck.

It took us a good half-hour to get the car out. We took turns standing in the snow in our sneakers with our shoulders against the bumper, pushing and rocking the car back and forth over the ice, until finally it roared free and we shouted our relief and joy into the icy night. Never mind that the muffler was making a strange growling, clattering sound all the way home. I'd worry about that later. At least the car worked, and that's all that mattered.

I got home around two a.m., paid Jessica almost an entire month's allowance for baby-sitting Rosie, and then slept in till noon on Saturday. That's when I woke up to Rosie standing by my bed, staring down at me with her hands on her hips. I must have felt those huge blue eyes boring into my skull, demanding that I wake up. Of course, she was already dressed in her white tights and pink leotard.

"I made you lunch," she told me.

"You can cook?" I asked with a yawn.

"I know how to make a baloney sandwich."

"Perfect," I said.

After lunch, we got in the car to go to Rosie's ballet lessons. When I turned the key in the ignition, the car growled like it was complaining, but at least it started, at least it ran.

"The car smells weird. And what's that funny sound?" Rosie asked me.

"Something going on with the muffler, I think. No big deal."

I shrugged at her, and she shrugged back. I figured I'd stop at the service station on the corner to get it fixed after I dropped off Rosie. Crap, what was that going to cost? After the baby-sitting and car repairs, last night was becoming way more expensive than it was worth.

"Are you coming to my recital next month, Danny?" Rosie asked over the muffler sounds as we pulled out of the driveway. "It's going to be really amazing."

"Yeah, of course," I said. "Have I ever missed one?"

Sure, three hours of little girls in tutus is a strange form of torture. But she came to my meets—which were also really long—and I went to her recitals. It was only fair.

"Okay, so my solo goes something like this," she said. Rosie pointed one of her pink sneakered feet at the windshield and swooped her arms around. "I'm this pretty white bird like a dove or something, who escapes from its cage and has to learn how to fly all over again because she forgot how, get it?"

"Got it."

The dance school was only about ten minutes away by car. All you needed to do was take a left turn out of our neighborhood, drive to the light at a major intersection, and go straight through it and over the hill into downtown Naperville.

The light turned red just as we approached the intersection. I pressed down on the brake, like I'd done hundreds of times. Only this time, nothing happened. My foot on the brake met no resistance, and the pedal went straight to the floor. The car didn't even slow down.

It barreled into the intersection, way too fast, after the crossing traffic had already begun to accelerate. A big gray truck headed straight for us.

Icy snow had scraped the hell out of the bottom of the car the night before. Metal on ice. Sharp smell in the garage—brake fluid draining. The twirling ballerina from the music box broke off, a terrible red wave crashed before my eyes, behind my eyes, everywhere.

No more, says the beast now at Walden Pond, the beast who has become my friend in spite of myself. My protector. Enough, he says.

Red turns to black, total eclipse, and I collapse behind a lichen-covered rock, far from home in the silent forest of Concord, Massachusetts.

13

THOMAS IS SITTING ON THE FRONT LANDING OF THE LIBRARY, waiting for me. I'm sure I look like crap, with dirt on my clothes, a sweat-stained shirt, and red eyes, but Thomas doesn't say a word about my appearance. Slowly, I climb the stairs to the concrete landing and collapse next to him, every muscle in my body on fire. We sit in silence, just watching the residents of Concord walk or jog by, generally enjoying the day. I envy them. So much.

"So, I suppose this is where you tell me you're not actually Thoreau reincarnated." Thomas says at last.

"Sorry to disappoint you," I say.

"It's okay. It was a crazy idea anyway. Would've been cool though."

"Yeah. Cool."

Thomas offers his water bottle to me, and I take a deep swig. The water is cold and feels good going down my dry throat.

"My name is Daniel," I tell him. "I live in Naperville, Illinois."

"Illinois? Wow, you're a long way from home." Thomas nods, salutes me with his water. "Pleased to meet you, Daniel."

I shake my head, and a dead maple leaf falls into my lap. "Well, you shouldn't be. I'm a really horrible person as it turns out."

Thomas considers this. "Try me."

I run my fingers through my hair, pull out pine needles, a dead moth. Then I turn to Thomas. My face is heavy and I feel about a hundred years old.

"My name is Daniel," I repeat. "I live in Illinois. And I think I killed my little sister."

Thomas pulls hard on his water bottle to mask his shock and swallows. "Why don't you start at the beginning and tell me what you found out."

But I can't speak. My head slumps forward and I'm afraid I'm going to start blubbering, right in front of Thomas.

"Hank," Thomas says. "Come on, let's find someplace more private to talk." He takes me to the side of the library, to a park bench partly hidden from the street by shrubs. We sit on the bench, and I lean over, stare at the ground, watch an ant carry off a breadcrumb. I wish I were an ant…or a breadcrumb.

"Hank, look at me," Thomas says.

So I do.

"Tell me about Daniel, but do me a favor, and tell me as Hank. Daniel is some kid I don't know, who had something bad happen to him, far away from here. I'd like to hear my friend Hank tell the story. Okay?"

I nod, wipe my stupid drippy nose with the palm of my hand.

"So there was this kid, Danny Henderson," I begin. My voice comes out all wobbly, so I clear my throat, take a deep breath, then continue. "He was one of those kids who just did what he was supposed to do, you know? He did his homework, ran track, pretty much did what his parents said and tried not to make trouble for anybody. I mean, sure, he partied with his friends and all, but I don't know, he just never got too crazy. Just a typical kid, trying to get by."

I tell him how Daniel went to the House of Blues in Chicago that night with Matt and Joey. How they crashed into a stupid snowbank and damaged the undercarriage of the car without even knowing it. How he and Rosie plowed into that intersection and couldn't stop. A big gray truck was coming, too fast.

Blood. Pink shoe.

A wave of dizziness breaks over me and without any warning, I barf right into the bushes next to the park bench. This is as far as the beast will let me go.

Everything that happened up to the accident is clear, but I can't remember the actual accident or the days after, except for a few sickening flashes. My memory goes straight from a gray truck bearing down on Mom's Toyota, to me sitting on the floor at Penn Station in New York City with Frankie staring into my face, saying, "You gonna eat that?"

Wiping my mouth miserably with the back of my hand, I choke out, "I don't even know if Rosie is alive or dead."

I'm afraid to see Thomas's response, expecting to see anger maybe or disgust. And I would deserve it. But instead, I see something that looks a whole lot like sadness. And even more amazing, sympathy.

"Hank," he says in a gentle voice. "You need to call your parents. No matter what happened that day, you have to call them and let them know you're okay."

"But I'm not okay!" I shout at Thomas.

"Of course you're not," he says quietly.

"God, Thomas. Why would they want anything to do with me ever again?"

Call your mother, Sophie said. *I guarantee she would sacrifice her own life just to have you home.*

How can I believe Thomas or Sophie? If I had one kid who killed or hurt another, I could never forgive that. There is not enough love and forgiveness in this world to make up for such a thing. Especially not after all my family has been through in the past five years. But I definitely can't talk about that.

"They're your parents. They love you."

"They love Rosie too," I argue back.

"Hank, they need to know where you are," Thomas says softly. "Facing up to this is better than running away."

No. Can't face it, not yet. What if I call and they tell me Rosie is dead? I almost puke into the bushes again, empty stomach seizing, and I just want to die. The beast still lives inside me, razor teeth and claws, resolute in protecting me from these final truths. I'm not ready yet. Threatening to swallow me into permanent forgetfulness, the beast insists that I run from this last horrible thing. For now.

I hide my face in my hands for a long time, smelling dead leaves and black dirt on my skin. Finally, I manage to say what Thomas wants to hear. "I'll call them," I say. "But after the weekend."

"No, Hank. My God. This must be torture for them. They need to know you're safe. And you need to know... about Rosie."

I fight the urge to curl up in a ball with my hands over my ears like some little kid in a nightmare. I just want to scream at Thomas to leave me alone, to understand that the bad stuff belongs to Danny, and I need to be Hank for just a little longer. "Thomas, three more days is not going to change anything," I say as evenly as possible through my clenched jaw. "I need to play for Hailey at the competition on Saturday. I can't let her down." Not one more person. Not Hailey.

Slowly, reluctantly, Thomas nods. "Okay, Hank. Three days," he says, holding up three fingers just in case I need the clarification. "And listen to me. You're not a bad kid. What happened back in Illinois, that was an accident."

"Thanks," I say, but I can see through the bullshit and platitudes. I've screwed up, and there's no way I can make it better. "Can you give me a ride back to your place, Thomas?" I ask. "I just need to lie down for a while."

In the parking lot, I climb on the back of Thomas's motorcycle, and as we ride to his house, I watch the horizon turn purple in the western sky. The end of another day in Concord, Massachusetts. And I know my days here are numbered.

That night, Thoreau visits me in the blue bedroom at Thomas's house. He's wearing his dark gray jacket and sitting in the same chair where Thomas was when I woke up that first morning here. Keeping vigil.

"So, now you know," he says.

"Yeah," I whisper into the half-dark. "Guess you knew all along."

He nods and tugs thoughtfully on his beard, which is longer than the last time I saw him and streaked with gray. Henry is older every time I see him. It's like he's slipping away from me, getting ready to leave me for good.

The thought of Henry leaving me now, just as I'm forced into the disaster that is my real life, makes me furious. God. I don't want pseudo-ghosts or dream visitations or whatever you'd call this. All I want is oblivion. Numbness. I'm not Thoreau reincarnated. Not even close. I'm just some screwed-up kid from Illinois who did something terrible and ran away. And he's just another crazy dream.

"Go away, Henry." I whisper.

He turns to look out the window into the sky, like he's trying to decide which star to inhabit in his next life. "You know where to find me," he says at last.

I turn my face toward the pillow, closing my eyes to the figure in the bedroom, denying him. When I open my eyes again, he's gone.

14

SOMEBODY IS HAMMERING ON THE DOOR. I ROLL OVER IN bed and bury my face in the pillow, ignoring the sound. Why doesn't Thomas answer his friggin' door? The doorbell rings next, and I open one bleary eye to see the sun glaring into the window from somewhere high in the sky, above the house. It's not morning anymore. What the hell time is it?

I have a vague memory of Thomas trying to wake me up earlier to take me with him to the library, but I told him to leave me alone so I could go back to sleep. It's all I want to do. Just stay in this bed with the covers over my head and sleep and sleep...and let the dreams come.

Mostly, they're memories in dream form, seeping back into my consciousness. Some of them are good—like remembering Christmases and birthdays. There was the year I got a new mountain bike and the time I got my first computer. And there were all those big holiday meals when my mom cooked a turkey, with grandparents and cousins crowded around the table. I dreamed about being in Boy Scouts and camping trips with my dad, mostly going up to Wisconsin into the north country, miles and miles from anybody and anything. Those were the best times of all.

The bad memory dreams are the ones where I see myself going through the motions of being a "good kid," when in truth I'm holding so much inside that I want to break furniture and throw things at the wall and scream until I burst a few blood vessels in my head. I'm the phoniest person around, putting hundreds of miles on my running shoes to escape, playing guitar till my calluses bleed because that's an escape too. On the outside, I'm the perfect kid—like a statue of perfect marble, serene and unreal. Inside, it's all snakes and maggots and broken glass.

And something else came to me in my dreams, something my whole family pretends to have amnesia about. I dreamed about Cole.

Closing my eyes against the sun, I try to go back to sleep.

The doorbell rings again, over and over, really insistently this time, and then I hear someone calling my name. A girl's voice. Uh-oh.

I get up and pull on a pair of jeans and pad barefoot to the front door, raking fingers through my wild bed hair. Open the door, and there she is.

"We have practice this afternoon. Did you forget?" It's Hailey, hair pulled back in a tight ponytail, car keys in her hand. One of her earrings is a dangly gold starfish, the other a seahorse. Her eyes snap with anger and I don't blame her. But then, when she gets a good look at me, her eyebrows crunch together in concern. "Hank, are you sick or something?"

Of course I forgot the band practice. With my memory banks under siege, I only have room for so much in my brain right now. But there's no way I can explain that to her without telling her everything.

"Hailey, I'm so sorry. I, uh, didn't sleep well last night and was just trying to catch up. What time is it?"

"Three thirty," she says, and her eyes blaze again. I was supposed to be at her house at three o'clock. "Sam and Ryan are already there. Are you coming or what?"

I don't know how to make any of this better other than to scramble and pull myself together and focus on her instead of my own pathetic life.

"Look, give me ten minutes to take a shower and get dressed, and I'll go with you. Ten minutes, I promise."

Hailey rolls her eyes and sits down in a wicker chair on the porch to wait for me, tossing her keys from one hand to the other.

After my shower, I comb my hair and peer at my face in the fogged-up mirror, trying not to see any trace of Danny there. When I'm with Hailey, there's no room for Danny. Only Hank.

The guys already have their gear set up in Hailey's basement when we arrive. Quickly, I hook up my guitar to the amp, and we start right in on our song. Even with the turmoil shredding my insides, I try to focus on the music. The smooth feel of the polished guitar under my hands. Electric buzz in my chest as I strum calloused fingers across the strings. My music, my escape.

As for the band, Sam is solid as always on the drums. Ryan, I don't know. The dude still struggles.

"I thought you were going to practice this at home," I say.

"I did," he says. "At least, I meant to. I had a whole lot of trig homework to do this week."

I shake my head. "Just do the best you can, okay? Let's go through this again."

After about the fifth time, he sounds a few degrees better. At least it's progress.

"Okay, you guys," Hailey says during a break. "Ms. Coleman asked me again about the name of our band. Any ideas?"

The room goes silent as we ponder this important detail.

"I know of this band called Seratonin. I always liked that name," Ryan says.

"Nah. That sounds too science geeky to me," Hailey says.

"Hailey and the Comets?" asks Sam. He smirks.

Hailey rolls her eyes. "I think that's been done, Sam."

"How about Carpe Diem?" I suggest. Everybody is quiet for a moment, thinking this over.

Carpe diem. It's the philosophy I want to embody. Seize the day. It's about putting all energy and attention into the present moment. This. Music and Hailey, and *now.* It's what Thoreau meant by sucking out the marrow of life, but it sounds way less grisly than something like Marrow Suckers. Although that could work too.

"Hm. Carpe Diem. I like that," Sam says. Slowly everybody nods in agreement.

"It's perfect," Hailey says and gives me this warm smile that shows me all is forgiven and she's crazy about me again.

Carpe Diem rocks into the song one more time and for once, even Ryan doesn't screw it up.

🌿

Hailey drops me off at "Uncle" Thomas's house just as it starts to get dark. She stops the car at the curb, turns off the motor, and turns to look at me.

"Is everything all right, Hank?" she asks.

No, Hailey. Things are not all right. They're bad, worse than you can imagine. "Well, I'm a little worried about Ryan." I'm amazed that my voice sounds calm, even with my insides shattered into a million pieces. "He keeps messing up the bridge, no matter how many times I remind him of the chords."

"He doesn't want to look like a fool up there. He'll get it." She taps the steering wheel with purple polished nails. "Are you worried about me too?"

"No," I say. She looks up at me, all hopeful, her eyes gleaming. "You have the most beautiful voice anybody is going to hear in that room on Saturday, Hailey. I know it, the band knows it, Ms. Coleman knows it. Anybody who's ever heard you sing knows it."

She wipes a tear from her cheek. "I feel so stupid," she says.

"You're not stupid, Hailey. Just take care of yourself this time." I rub the back of my index finger across her soft cheek. "And if you get scared, just pretend it's you and me, me and you, all alone in the white room, making music."

Hailey tucks her arm into mine, snuggles her face into my shoulder. "Yeah. I like that. You and me, me and you," she murmurs. "Maybe it'll be okay after all."

"Of course it will." I lean my head against hers, breathe in the clean shampoo smell of her hair, trying to memorize every detail of this moment. I could love this girl so easily. If only I could be normal and allow that to happen.

Hailey nuzzles her cheek against my shirt in silence for a moment, then gazes up at me as if she's trying to read me with those intense gold-flecked eyes. "What else is wrong, Hank? I know there's something. Talk to me, please?"

So here it is. My chance to tell Hailey everything. To let her, for real, into the chaos that is my life. She slips a warm hand into my sweaty one and squeezes. I squeeze back until I'm afraid I'll crush her hand, and I let go.

"You've always had this evasive, mysterious thing about you that's kind of sexy, but it's different now," she says. "To tell the truth, it's scaring me a little."

Oh, Hailey. It would be such a sweet relief to let her hold me and tell me it'll be okay. But what am I supposed to say? That I'm a loser criminal who robbed and assaulted some guy in New York and maybe killed my sister in a car accident that was totally my fault? She'd probably run away screaming and be afraid of me forever. How can I possibly tell her who I really am or what I've done?

God, I'm tired. No more fight in me, no more strength. Hailey and music are the only good, pure things in my life right now. I can't spoil them too. Everything will turn to shit soon enough.

"Look, these next few days are all about you and the music, Hailey. Let's just enjoy them, okay? After that, we'll talk and I'll tell you everything. I promise. Okay?" I'm not even sure what I mean by *after that*. Anything that might happen after the Battle of the Bands is a huge void. My future is as blank and formless as my past used to be. So I'm buying time, just a couple more days.

She nods reluctantly, and before she can speak, I give her a soft kiss, hoping she doesn't notice my lips trembling.

"See you tomorrow, Hailey." Then I get out of the car and gently shut the door.

♦

It's Thursday and I'm at the library shelving nonfiction on the second floor, breathing in that old book smell. I figured I might as well live these last days in Concord as normally as possible. Doing work makes me feel something like a normal person with some kind of normal purpose. It's hard to stay focused, though. I have to re-shelve a whole pile of books I stuffed into the biography section, when actually they belong in history. Whatever.

One more day until the Battle of the Bands. And after Saturday night, I promised Thomas I would call my parents and face the truth about what happened in Naperville. Face the truth about New York City. Like, what about the crimes I committed? Will the police conclude I was acting in self-defense when I clobbered Simon with that brick? Of course I fled the scene of a crime, and that doesn't look good. And I did take the guy's money. Indirectly, but I still took it.

Even if they don't throw me in jail, then what? It's not like I'll just be able to return to my old life. It's impossible to imagine going home, sleeping in my old bed, going to my old school, and trying to reconnect with friends. Aside from all the bad stuff, I've missed a lot of school, so I doubt I can graduate with my class in May. Not that it matters.

My parents don't know this yet, but I'm not going to college. The day the acceptance letter came from Northwestern University, I hid it in the back of my sock drawer and went out for a ten-mile run. I didn't think of anything at all for the first five miles except my body moving and sneakers pounding on the asphalt. But finally my mind cleared enough to realize the cold, hard, honest truth: I don't want to go to college. Not yet, anyway. A few days before the accident, I even called the college and told them I was delaying college for a year so I could figure out what I wanted to do. They were actually really nice about it. But my parents, no doubt about it, they're going to be pissed.

God. My head is spinning. So much for normal.

When I finish shelving, I slump down in a chair next to Thomas, my long legs kicked out in front of me, exhausted more from the war zone in my head than the work.

"You okay, Hank?"

I shrug. "Just need to sit for a while."

So I do, just listening to the clock in the library, to

Thomas typing on his keyboard, absorbing the quiet, the peacefulness of this particular moment in time, this now.

"I wish you'd been right," I say after a while.

"About what?"

"About me being Thoreau reincarnated," I say.

Thomas grins at me. "Me too. I had a lot of questions I wanted to ask you."

I lean back in the chair, gaze over at the statue of Thoreau near Thomas's desk. "Do you really think somebody could live like him today?"

"Sure. People do it all the time. There are people in the northwest, like in Montana, living off the grid right now. Of course there's a lot more grid these days than when Thoreau was around."

"There's no way a reincarnated Thoreau would choose to live at Walden Pond now," I say. "Just the sound of the traffic on Route Two would drive him crazy."

"You got that right."

"So if Henry lived today, where would he go?"

Thomas grins at me like he's been hoping forever for someone to ask that very question. "This won't surprise you, but I've given that a lot of thought. And I have the answer for you."

"I thought you might."

He gets up and goes over to a nearby shelf. Peers at

the titles through his glasses, then pulls one of the books out and hands it to me.

I look down at the title, *The Maine Woods* by Henry David Thoreau.

"Maine," says Thomas. "It's a huge state, and there are still thousands of acres that are real wilderness."

"He was there?"

"Yep, he took several trips up there, when a lot of it was still unmapped and uncharted. It might have been a bit much for Henry back then. Here. Listen to this." Peering through his glasses, he licks a finger and starts flipping through the book.

He clears his throat, reads in a hushed, library-worthy, but dramatic voice: *"I stand in awe of my body, this matter to which I am bound has become so strange to me. I fear not spirits, ghosts, of which I am one,—that my body might,— but I fear bodies, I tremble to meet them. What is this Titan that has possession of me? Talk of mysteries!— Think of our life in nature,—daily to be shown matter, to come in contact with it,—rocks, trees, wind on our cheeks! The solid earth! the actual world! the common sense! Contact! Contact! Who are we? where are we?"*

I take this in, snort out a little laugh. "Wow. Sounds like Henry was freaked."

"Definitely. He wrote this when he was near the

summit of Mount Katahdin, the highest point in Maine. We're talking true wilderness, the tail end of the Appalachian Trail, the real deal. Concord was a luxury vacation in the Bahamas compared to this."

I imagine Thoreau standing on this mountaintop in Maine, not the cocky, cranky guy from Concord I've gotten to know, but someone out of place, completely amazed by his surroundings. Scared and humbled by his own existence on the planet.

"I keep meaning to go to Maine, retrace Thoreau's steps, with a canoe and camping gear. I even went out and bought a tent and backpack but never got around to going. One of these days." He flips through the book, gazes at pictures of sweeping vistas from the top of Mount Katahdin. "You know, sometimes I wonder if it bugged him that he never actually reached the summit. He was close, and at the time he thought he made it. I guess that's what's important." Thomas shrugs. "Anyway, guess we'll never know." He hands the book to me. "Here, read it. A modern-day Thoreau could kick ass in the Maine woods."

I run my fingers over the picture on the cover, thinking of woods and waterfalls and acres of true wildness far away from the sounds of a highway or a train or best of all, people.

15

Hiking the Appalachian Trail—all 2,181 miles of it, from Georgia to Maine—was something my Dad and I used to talk about all the time. It was like all our other camping trips were just training runs for the real thing, the ultimate hike we would take. Someday.

This is probably one of my last nights in Concord, and I'm sitting on a moss-covered tree trunk on the banks of Walden Pond. I watch the purple and pink of the sunset reflect in the smooth surface of the water, try to empty my mind and let Walden do its magic. This is where I started and this is where I'd like to end, but better equipped this time. On a rock behind me sits a backpack containing my supplies for the night: A blue sleeping bag I borrowed from Thomas, breakfast food inside a plastic container to keep animals away, and extra layers of clothes in case it gets cold.

Just being here, ready for a campout, reminds me of the last camping trip I went on with my dad.

It was last summer in Hayward, Wisconsin, way up by the Minnesota border. We found this great campsite right on Lake Chippewa. I remember that day so clearly, kicking back in camp chairs, Dad cooking burgers over the campfire while I paged through one of my hiking magazines in the fading daylight. I remember everything we said and did, like it's a movie in my head.

"Hey, Dad, I found this article with a list of potential hazards on the Appalachian Trail," I said to him. "You want to hear it?"

"Of course." He flipped the burgers with a spatula and sent grease sizzling into the fire. "We need to be prepared."

"Okay, let's see. 'Mosquitoes, biting flies, poison ivy,'" I read out loud. "Are you kidding me? You call those hazards?"

"I don't know. Poison ivy all over your face and body and nether regions? I'd call that a hazard," Dad pointed out.

"Yeah, but come on. Just wear heavy duty bug repellent and stay away from shiny three-leafed plants. That's like Hiking 101."

"You'd be surprised how many boneheads think they can hike the trail and don't know what they're getting into." Dad took off his Chicago Cubs cap, the one he wore all summer long because he thought it would give our team luck, although it seemed to have the opposite effect. He scratched his head and smashed the cap back down. Black hair stuck out in tufts over his ears.

I scanned the rest of the list. "'Severe weather,' duh. 'Steep grades,' also duh. Ah, now we're talking. 'American black bear' and 'venomous snakes.' Those are hazards I can respect. Oh, and here's the last one: 'Diarrhea from drinking water.'" I glanced up at my dad. "Seriously?"

"Hm. Black bears and diarrhea. I'm scared already. Maybe we better just pitch a tent in the backyard."

Dad scooped the burgers onto buns I'd set out on metal camping plates and handed me mine.

"We should definitely do it." Dad took a big bite of his burger. "Hike the Appalachian Trail."

"Well, yeah," I said. "We've been talking about it since I was twelve."

"I know, but I think it's time we actually made some plans."

I stopped mid-chew to stare at my dad. "For real?" To tell the truth, I always figured the Appalachian Trail was a dream we liked to talk about, but that would never happen. After all, it's over 2,000 miles long and crosses through fourteen states. To do that on foot would take an entire summer at least. There's no way my dad would take that much time off work.

"For real."

"When?" I popped the last bite of burger into my mouth.

"Next summer, after you graduate from high school. That would be a great way to celebrate, don't you think?"

"Well, hell yeah. That would be amazing. Let's do it."

The Appalachian Trail meant hiking through the woods of Georgia, North Carolina, Tennessee, and finishing up in Vermont, New Hampshire, and Maine. The hike itself would be incredibly cool. Also, for the rest of my life, even when I was old, I could work into conversations, *Now that reminds me of the time back in the day when I hiked the Appalachian Trail.*

"It would be a great way for us to spend some quality time together before you head off to college." Dad threw another log on the campfire. The embers crackled and jumped.

College. This was the last thing I wanted to think

about. Contemplating my future was like peering into a black hole. But Dad had expectations. College is just what people did. Everyone should have it all worked out by age eighteen: a list of goals, a total life plan. Yeah, right. I was terrified to tell anybody this, but I didn't have a plan. I didn't even have a clue.

"So, have you started your applications?" He tried to sound casual, but I was losing him. He was switching from Dad, my camping buddy, to Dad, the parent who knows what's best, the one who says I better step up or obviously I'll be a major disappointment. A subtle shift, but it was there, loud and clear. "It would be a good idea to get started on your essay this summer."

"I know, Dad. Look, can we talk about something else?" I started to feel sick, dinner churning in my stomach.

"But, Danny, you need to get serious about—" Dad began.

"Yes, I know, Dad. 'Danny, it's time get serious about your future, your education, your career, blah blah blah.' But it's not like you can squeeze all your wise fatherly advice into one week and then disappear on another business trip."

I felt bad as soon as I said it, but it was the truth. He was always out on the road even, I suspected, when he didn't need to be.

Dad stared into the fire. He didn't even try to deny it. "I'm sorry, son."

Neither of us said a thing for a long time, just watched the wood burn down into glowing red coals as the sky grew darker. Crickets and cicadas started their night sounds and fireflies flashed signals in the tall grass by the pond. When I finally spoke, what I had to say came out so low I wasn't sure he could hear me. Or if I even wanted him to.

"Dad, how come we never talk about Cole?"

He drew in a quick breath. For both of us, hearing the name out loud felt like a blow to the heart. "You know why, Danny."

"No, Dad, I don't."

He took his hat off and raked fingers through his hair. "It's your mother," he said. "She feels responsible for what happened. I thought you knew that."

"How could I know when we don't talk about it? It's like Cole never existed."

Tears prickled behind my eyes then, as they do now, as I sit by the edge of Walden Pond and remember.

When I close my eyes, I can still see Cole that last morning when I glanced back at the house on my way to school. He was standing at the living room window like he did every day, wearing his Batman pajamas and waving good-bye.

Everybody said he looked exactly like I did when I was two, with his gray eyes and hair all black and thick like mine.

That afternoon, when the guidance counselor came to get me, we were working on the isosceles triangle theorem in eighth grade geometry class. He whispered something in my teacher Mrs. Pearson's ear, and then they both looked over at me. Somehow I knew something bad had happened, like a premonition.

At the funeral, everybody talked about what a terrible tragedy it was. An accident. Mom had been working on the garden like she did every May, planting flowers around the pool fence. Cole was doing what he called "helping," using a beach shovel and a Tonka dump truck to push dirt around.

When the phone rang that day, Mom picked Cole up and carried him into the house with her. But when she went looking for a pen and paper to write something down, he ran back outside, probably to get his truck. He loved that truck, partly because it was my favorite truck when I was little, and I gave it to him. By the time Mom finished the call and realized he wasn't playing at her feet like she'd thought, Cole had opened the closed gate around the pool—we still don't know how he did that—got too close to the edge, and slipped silently into the deep end, still holding on to that truck.

Cole would've turned seven years old this year and been a second-grader, but his life ended the year I turned thirteen and Rosie was four. He drowned in the pool at our house in Evanston, and Mom was so devastated that we had to move. In fact, we moved three times in five years, each time to another house in a different suburb. On the outside, every one of those houses was really pretty. But inside those houses, nothing changed. Mom was drinking, Dad was leaving, and Rosie and I were trying to be perfect. No matter how many times we moved, we were still us. And to be honest, it wasn't working out so well.

"Are you and Mom getting a divorce?" I whispered to my dad by the campfire that night in Wisconsin, unable to be silent on that too.

Dad looked down at his hands, rubbing dirt off his knuckles. "I'm...not sure. It's complicated, Danny. I don't expect you to understand."

He was right. I didn't understand why my family's world continued to fall apart and I was completely powerless over everything. Whether it was fair or not, I blamed my father for not making it better. He was the dad, and it was his job to make it better. Without another word, I unrolled my sleeping bag by the fire, turned away, and pretended to go to sleep. We didn't talk about hiking the Appalachian Trail again for the rest of that trip. In fact, neither of us ever brought it up again.

❧

At Walden Pond my thoughts are full of these things I'd forgotten. Like losing Cole and fighting with Dad. Camping and the Appalachian Trail.

If Cole had lived, we would've taken him camping, and I would've shown him how to do everything—like build campfires, find stars and planets in the night sky, and hunt for wild blueberries. But I never got a chance to show him much of anything.

Picking up flat stones on the shores of the pond, I chuck them at an angle and they skim across the surface, five, six, seven times. I was a rock-skipping champ. I would've taught Cole how to do that too.

I pick up a couple more stones from the edge of the water and examine them on my open palm. One is a perfect oval of quartz, smooth and white. The other is a chunk of gray granite, with rough edges and tiny mirrors of mica in it.

Maybe if I'm lucky, Thoreau will visit me in my dreams, so I can talk to him one more time. Sounds goofy, but I really want to know: if he were in my place, What Would Henry Do? Would he go home and face the mess he left behind? Or would he strike out on his own, start a new life and never look back?

A few feet away from Thoreau's cabin site is a huge pile of rocks called a cairn that has been growing on this spot for decades. People who visit the site place rocks on the cairn, basically to honor Thoreau, acknowledging that he was somebody special, to say hey Henry, whassup, I was here to see you.

I set my gray stone on top of the pile gently, like a sign of respect. Or a good-bye. The smooth white stone I slip into my pocket, a tiny souvenir of Walden to take with me, wherever I end up next.

Then, instead of settling myself on the hearth of Thoreau's former cabin like that first night, I find a dry, hidden spot to lay out the sleeping bag behind a boulder. The warmer weather has attracted a lot of random hikers, and I don't want any company. Hopefully I'm still close enough for the spirit of Thoreau to know I'm here.

Please come, Henry. Please. I need to talk to you.

The minutes tick by, but time seems to pass slower here in the woods. The sky is sprinkled with a million stars, and the pines are silhouetted against the deep blue stretching over my head. An owl hoots from somewhere high in an oak tree. Some small animal rustles in the bushes at the shore of the pond. A mosquito whines in my ear.

I wait. And wait. The night stretches on before me and all around me, envelops me. It's also waiting but for nothing, it turns out, other than itself.

❦

A loud chorus of singing, twittering, trilling birds wakes me up the next morning, and I duck my head inside the sleeping bag to muffle the sound, but it does no good. The birds have decided it's time to get up, and it's pointless to try to get more sleep. Okay, okay. I'm up already.

Thoreau never came last night. There was no visit, no dreams. Nothing. I avoid the chilly morning air by hunkering down in the sleeping bag with only my hair sticking out of the top, listening to the songs of all the birds, like a crazy orchestra tuning up. Here in the woods, I can almost convince myself that my problems in the human world don't even exist. Which is maybe what Henry has been saying all along. *Simplicity, simplicity, simplicity*. Don't take more from the world than you need. Don't need more than you take. Somehow nature puts things into perspective.

"What the—are you kidding me? Hey, kid! Get back here with my stuff!"

From somewhere near the pond, I hear a guy's voice thundering into the woods. At first I think he's shouting at me, which makes no sense. Then I hear someone crash past me in the underbrush, not ten feet away. Popping my head out of the sleeping bag, I see some kid in a plaid coat, red scarf, and black knit cap pulled down low over his head running up the hill, a bundle in his arms. I scramble out of the sleeping bag and stand up to get a better look.

There, in the clearing by Thoreau's cabin site, is a guy with bushy red hair, dripping with pond water, wearing nothing but a pair of drenched boxers and shivering with cold and fury. The guy breaks into a clumsy, bare-footed run into the woods after the thief who apparently stole his clothes. After running just a few yards, he bellows in pain, grabs his foot, and unleashes an amazing tirade of creative cursing about what he intends to do to the thief, his entire extended family, and any domestic animals they happen to own. I'm so impressed that I just stand there, staring.

Spotting me there beside the boulder, the guy actually shakes his fist at me and says, "What are you just standing there for? Stop that bastard now, for the love of God!" He gestures toward the crashing figure, swiftly disappearing into the woods.

The insult and indignity of the guy's situation strikes me. Besides, what else am I going to do, say, *Nah, you're on your own. You just stand there and freeze your ass off. I don't care?* Of course not. So I step out of the sleeping bag, slip on my sneakers without lacing them, and bound into the woods after the kid who was cruel enough to steal a half-naked guy's clothes when he was looking the other way.

The thief has grown momentarily silent, maybe realizing that twigs breaking and dead leaves crunching under his feet give away his location. He must be hiding now, crouched behind a bush or a large rock.

But then I spot his red knit scarf, caught in a branch near his hiding place by a toppled pine tree, and all hell breaks loose as he gives in to the chase. He ducks behind a stand of maple trees, but I spot him at the top of the hill, trying to find a shortcut out to the street.

"Hey you, stop!" I shout, which is stupid of course, because this only makes him run faster. He stumbles on a branch, almost falls, and I finally gain on him. Reaching the back of his coat, I grab on, tackle him to the ground, and we somersault together in the leaves. I roll him over, pin him down on the dirt with my knees on his shoulders, and get a good look at him.

Huge blue eyes stare up at me, the bottom half of his face covered by the flipped-up collar of the plaid coat. A strand of long blond hair sneaks out from under the wool hat. Whoa, whoa, whoa. Wait a minute. This is no guy. It's a girl.

"Sorry," I stammer, all embarrassed, until I remind myself she's a thief, even if she is female, with long blond hair and pretty eyes. "I mean, come on, who steals a guy's clothes?"

The girl blinks at me, dark lashes, eyes that look familiar somehow.

"Hank?" she says.

"Nessa?" My voice comes out something like a squeak. Stunned, I scramble to my feet away from her, and with her hands freed, she yanks the hat off her head, pulls the collar away from her face, and I see her huge smile.

"Hank!" she cries out, and she's throwing her arms around my neck, practically jumping all over me. "I found you!"

Nessa is here, hanging off my neck, here in Concord, Massachusetts, and I'm too startled to convert any of the questions in my head into coherent sentences. I register that she's a blond now—after the makeover Magpie ordered—and that although she's still pretty, her hands, face, and clothes are filthy.

"Yes, you found me," I say at last. "I...here you are, and I have so many questions about that." I shake my head to

234

clear it, like shaking off a crazy dream that makes no sense. "But you know, there's a guy standing down there shivering in his underwear, and he needs his clothes back."

She grins, but lowers her eyes like she's at least making an attempt to be ashamed. "I'm sorry," she says.

"Look, just give me his clothes," I say. "I'll tell him you got away, but that you dropped all his stuff. Okay?"

She shrugs, then nods. "Okay, Hank." Before I can scoop up the clothes, she grabs my hand, her blues eyes searching my face. "Promise you'll come back?" She's squeezing my fingers so hard it actually hurts. "Please?"

"Of course, I will. I promise."

Nessa helps me gather up a denim shirt, black jeans, a pair of cowboy boots, and a backpack, and I jog down the hill to where the guy is pacing around the clearing with a limp, his arms wrapped around his chest, shivering even harder now, his lips turning blue. Close up, I can see the guy is older than I thought, probably in his forties. He has thick red hair on his chest and back, almost like fur, but it's obviously not enough to keep him warm on a chilly spring morning in New England.

"The kid got away." I tell him. "But the good news is that he dropped your stuff. Here."

He grabs the bundle of clothes, and he's still cursing like crazy under his breath, not that I blame him. He looks so funny, I have to bite the inside of my cheek to keep from smiling.

"All I wanted to do was come to Walden Pond and emulate Thoreau by taking a morning bath in these sacred waters like he did," the guy murmurs, eyes still blazing. "But then some asshole runs off with my gear. I bet *that* never happened to Thoreau."

Emulating Thoreau, eh? I look at his drenched boxers. They're pink, covered with red and white hearts, like joke underwear his wife or girlfriend gave him for Valentine's Day. *Nice boxers*, I almost say out loud.

As if reading my thoughts, the guy blushes and pulls his pants on, right over his wet underwear. "Okay then," I say, hoping to spare either of us both further embarrassment. "Sorry this happened to you. Have a good day now." I turn away, still fighting a smile.

"Wait," he says hastily, and I turn back. "Uh, thanks. You did a good thing."

You did a good thing. A good thing. Well, that's nice for a change.

I grab my sleeping bag from behind the boulder, stuff it into the pack and swing it onto my back before heading up to join Nessa. I find her right where I left her, sitting cross-legged on the ground, ripping the bark off a dead branch.

"Hank," she says, nodding as if to reassure herself. "You came back."

"Of course I did."

She sighs, a deep inhale and exhale that racks her small body. Then tears start rolling down her face, leaving tracks in the dirt. Damn. I hate to see a girl cry. It just makes me want to go find the person who hurt her and beat him up.

"What's going on, Nessa?"

"It's Jack," she says in a whisper. "He's hurt, bad."

"Where is he?"

She scrambles to her feet and grabs my hand with icy fingers. "I'll take you."

Holding my hand tight like a little girl, Nessa leads me through the woods and down to the path, then over fallen trees and new spring undergrowth, to a hiding place on the other side of the pond.

"We came to Concord to look for you," she says, anticipating my questions. "You left us plenty of clues, like your name. Henry David. Jack remembered that. And he remembered the book you showed him, *Walden*, and how you said it was a clue to who you are. It wasn't hard to do a little research and find out where Walden is. We figured if we hung around here long enough, you might just show up. Which you did."

"But why did you steal that guy's stuff?"

Nessa's face is dirty, but a red flush shows through. "I just happened to walk by and saw clothes and thought maybe there was food in that pack. We need clean clothes and we're hungry. Do you blame me?"

I shrug. Doesn't matter now. Plus, it's not like I can judge stealing after all the laws I've broken in the past few weeks. "So why did you leave New York? And what happened to Jack?"

Nessa pulls the black hat down over her ears. "Things got bad with Magpie, so we had to get out of there." she says. "He was really mad after you left, even though Jack told him he tried to stop you from leaving. But he was pissed at both of us. I thought he liked us, that he wanted to take care of us, but he got so mean. He started getting meaner and meaner. He started hurting Jack almost every day. And then, me."

"Magpie was hurting you?" I ask Nessa. She nods, not meeting my eyes. All I want to do is take Magpie by his proper English neck and squeeze the proper English life right out of him.

"The worst was a couple days ago. Magpie sent Jack to collect a debt from one of his clients. The guy wouldn't pay. But when Jack came back empty-handed, Magpie didn't believe him. He got so mad he beat Jack up. I think he broke his arm." Tears streak down Nessa's dirty cheeks. "I was so upset, I went to the client myself and made him give me the money." I don't even want to know how she managed that, so I don't ask. "But then Jack and I ran away. There's no way either of us was going back."

"You mean, you stole the money from Magpie?"

"The way we saw it, he owed it to us. Every penny."

"Somehow, I don't think he'd see it that way," I say. A realization dawns on me. "Hey, did you come looking for me at the high school? Did you ask a lady janitor about me?"

"Yeah. Jack thought he saw you walk into the school. I didn't think the guy looked like you, but Jack is not always so clear on stuff these days."

So it was Nessa, dressed as a boy, and Jack, who came looking for me and talked to Sophie. Not Magpie or any of the scary guys who work for him. I'm safe. Maybe we're all safe.

"Jack was in so much pain the whole way." Nessa leads me off the path to push through some thicker under-brush. She swipes at her nose with the end of her scarf. "I had to give him something."

"Like what?"

"Something for the pain."

"Jesus, Nessa."

"They were pills. I don't know what kind. Magpie gave them to us, and we were going to sell them. But Jack needed some."

Shit. This keeps getting worse. I have no idea what I'm going to find when I finally lay eyes on Jack.

We skirt around a thick oak tree and see their hiding place under the ledge of a huge lichen-covered rock. Jack is there, and at first, I swear he looks dead lying there on a bed of brown leaves, his worn army jacket laid over him like a blanket. Sleeping with his mouth open, he looks six instead of sixteen. Nessa kneels next to him in the leaves and rests a hand on his shoulder. I drop my pack on the ground and stand looking down at them both, feeling helpless.

"Jack, I found him. I found Hank," she says softly. Nothing. He doesn't even twitch. "C'mon, Jack, wake up." She jiggles his shoulder, but he's motionless. We lock eyes. Did they make it all the way here to Walden only for Jack to overdose and die here in the woods? Nessa shakes him again, harder this time.

"Fuck!" Jack jolts straight up, his eyes bulging. We rear back, taken totally off guard. "Goddamn, Nessa," he moans, falling back into the leaves. "That's my sore arm."

"I'm sorry, I'm so sorry," she murmurs, tears flooding

her eyes. "I...I found Hank. I brought him here."

Jack holds his arm close to his chest like it's a broken wing, eyes screwed shut against the pain. Then takes a couple deep breaths before looking up to acknowledge my presence.

"Hey, ugly," he says at last, like the first time we met, and I almost smile. But his voice is weak and slurred, and there's a purple bruise on his cheekbone.

"How you feeling, Jack?"

He winces. "Terrible, man. I think my arm's broke. Magpie—"

"Yeah, I know. Nessa told me."

He needs help. But here we are, way off the path in Walden Woods, too far from the road for a car to get in. And there's no way I'll be calling an ambulance or alerting the park rangers.

"Can you eat, Jack? You hungry?"

"Always hungry."

I reach into my backpack and pull out the food I brought along for breakfast. "Here. You're even skinnier than the last time I saw you. Eat this."

I hand him a couple glazed doughnuts and open a container of apple juice. He wolfs the doughnuts down like he hasn't eaten in days. Nessa eats one and lets Jack devour the rest.

"Okay, Jack, this is what we're going to do," I tell him. "Nessa and I are going to help you walk out of the woods, and we'll find a place for you to sit, closer to the street. Then I'm going to go get help."

"No, Hank." Even though he's sick and hurt, there's no doubt Jack would attack like a rabid dog if he felt cornered. "We didn't come all this way for you to get us sent back to our fucking father."

He scratches at his face like he wants to peel off his own skin, and Nessa starts to whimper again. I pull his hands from his face.

"Jack, relax. I promise that won't happen. I have friends here, and I trust them. One is a nurse. She helped me when I was sick, and she'll help you."

"We don't have a choice," Nessa whispers gently to Jack. "We can't go back to New York. We have to trust Hank."

Jack gives me a long look that flickers between suspicion and hope. "Okay," he says at last.

I stuff my backpack under a rocky ledge and make a mental note of its location so I can pick it up later. Then together, Nessa and I help Jack to his feet. I pull my own coat over his shoulders as he cradles his injured arm. His other arm, I drape around my neck.

The three of us stagger through the woods near the beginning of the path to Walden Pond, not far from the parking area. "Stay here," I say. "I'll be back with my friends as soon as I can. Don't go anywhere. Promise?"

The two of them sit down on a stone wall near the beach area of the pond. Jack stares hollow-eyed into the shallow water, clearly surrendering to whatever might be next.

"Right. Where else we gonna go?"

❧

"Sweetie, I'm so sorry, but this is going to hurt," says Suzanne in a soft voice.

Jack is lying on the green leather couch in Thomas's living room. Suzanne kneels in front of him with his injured arm cradled in her hands, while Nessa, Thomas, and I stand nearby, feeling useless. Still dressed in the blue scrubs she wore during her overnight shift at the hospital, Suzanne is in total nurse mode.

"The good news is that your arm isn't broken," she says. "The bad news is that it's dislocated, and getting the joint back in place takes some messing around with your sore shoulder. Ready?"

Jack's face is white and his eyes look enormous in his thin face, but he nods. Nessa buries her face in my shoulder as Suzanne takes hold of Jack's arm, pulls it toward her, then pushes back. Jack howls in pain, but through gritted teeth, says, "Do it," so Suzanne does. With a sick, audible pop, his shoulder slips back into its socket.

"Better?" asks Suzanne.

"Yeah," says Jack in a strangled whisper. Nessa lets out a deep breath into my chest and I feel the heat of it through my shirt.

Suzanne folds a big black bandana into a triangle and knots it around Jack's neck to create a sling. Gently, she tucks his arm into it and presses it against his chest.

"It's still going to hurt for a while, Jack. But you should feel better in a few days."

Jack closes his eyes without responding, and Thomas pulls an afghan off the back of the couch and spreads it over Jack's body. He looks so small just lying there with the fight drained out of him, but I know it's temporary. Jack's a fighter. He'll be back.

"Get some sleep now, buddy," Thomas says.

Suzanne turns to Nessa. "So, Nessa," she says, using her nice-nurse-lady voice, like she's talking to a five-year-old. "Would you like to take a nap too or maybe a bath?"

After all the sick adult stuff Nessa has been through on the streets, it probably feels good to have somebody speak to her like she's a child. She smiles and I get a glimpse of the girl she might be if she'd had a normal life. "Both, please," she says. "Can I have the bath first?"

Suzanne leads Nessa upstairs. We hear them discuss bubbles versus bath salts, whatever those are, and Nessa sounds so happy being normal, just being a kid and a girl.

Thomas juts his chin toward the kitchen. "Coffee?" he asks me.

"Sure." We go in, and I sit down at the nicked wood table.

He pours a cup for me in a blue mug that says *The Thoreau Society* on the side. Hands it to me with a tight smile.

"I'm sorry, Thomas," I say, low enough that Jack won't hear me, if he's even awake enough to listen. "I didn't know they'd follow me here."

"Well," he says slowly, and I can tell he's being cautious. It was one thing for Thomas to help me out, but another to take in my messed-up friends. "Obviously, they need help."

"Yeah, they do." I think of the bruises on Jack's face, remember Nessa crying in the shack behind the Dumpster that first night. And Magpie's cruel smile. "They really do."

Suzanne comes downstairs and joins us in the kitchen. "Poor thing. She's filthy. I put her in the tub for a nice, long soak. I just hope she doesn't fall asleep in there."

After pouring herself a cup of coffee, she joins us at

the table, adds a spoonful of sugar to her coffee, and stirs while we watch in numb silence. "So, Hank, we need to call somebody. You know that, right?"

Alarm prickles my scalp. "Like who?"

"Child services."

"They can't be sent back to their dad. He was abusing them."

Thomas's eyes harden and his big, callused hands flex unconsciously into fists on the table. If he knew the whole story, he'd want to smack more than a few people around. The thought of Thomas in warrior mode is weirdly comforting.

"Would they have to go back home?" I ask. "I mean, if the authorities knew they were here?"

"Not if there's abuse," Suzanne says. "They might be placed in a foster home."

Thomas clenches his jaw and his temple throbs. "That's not always the best solution either."

"Not always," she agrees, and I can tell by the way she covers one of his fists with her hand that she knows at least something about his past. "But it's better than being on the streets."

"They can't go out on the streets again," I say, thinking of Magpie and all the other potential Magpies out there. "There's no way."

Suzanne takes a thoughtful sip of coffee. "There are programs through the hospital to help kids like them. Let me make a few calls."

"Okay, thanks," I say, wondering how I could ever fully thank them for everything. After draining my coffee cup, I excuse myself and go into the living room to check on Jack.

"You okay, dude?"

Jack opens one slitted eye and groans.

"So sorry about the shoulder, Jack," I say. "That really sucks."

"Hank," he says through teeth tight with pain. He shoots a glance toward the kitchen and then waves me closer so I'll lean in to listen to his lowered voice. "It's not just my arm. Need some pills. Just a little Oxy would do it. Or Xanax. Please, Hank?" He holds out a pleading hand, and I can see how badly it's shaking. "Something, anything," he murmurs.

"Can't do it, buddy." I feel that familiar dark urge to wrap my hands around Magpie's neck and squeeze, because I'm sure he's the one who got Jack hooked. It's possible Jack was even an addict when I first met him, but I didn't recognize the signs. "I'm sorry."

The only thing I can do for Jack now is just be with him and be his friend. So I collapse into an overstuffed chair and watch over him as he shivers and twitches and eventually falls asleep. Laying my head back, I close my eyes and start to doze off too. I'm exhausted after my restless night in the woods and everything that happened at Walden after I woke up.

Funny, I went looking for Thoreau and found Jack and Nessa instead. And that's good, I guess. But I can't help wondering if I'll ever see Henry again.

16

HAILEY LOOKS SMOKING HOT WHEN SHE DRIVES OVER TO pick me up for the Battle of the Bands that night. Smudged black lines around her eyes make them smoky and sexy, and she's wearing this tight black outfit and black leather boots that make her look like a rock star, or maybe Catwoman. Like I said, hot.

"Hailey, you're gorgeous." I give her a kiss. Her lips are trembling. So are her earrings, one a red feather, the other black. "You're going to kick ass tonight."

She smiles and reaches over to wipe her red lipstick off my mouth. "You too," she says. But her fingers, shiny with black nail polish, are shaking as they grip the steering wheel. She pulls the keys out of the ignition and holds them out to me with a pleading expression. "Will you drive, Hank? I'm too nervous."

Automatically I accept the keys, but my blood turns to ice. The last time I drove a car was that day with Rosie, the day of the accident. Just the feel of the keys forces the bitter smell of brake fluid into my sinuses and I see the gray truck coming for us before the memory shuts down. I'm so dizzy I want to rest my head on the dashboard for a while, but I don't. Forcing the memories away, I cram them into a closet and slam the door.

Today is about Hailey. I have to pull Hailey through this night before I can consider my own ruined life. So we switch seats and I get behind the wheel like everything's cool, turn the key, put my foot on the brake, and adjust the rearview mirror. Then I turn up the classic rock radio station—some rocking tune by Aerosmith— and give Hailey a cheesy double thumbs-up to show her all is well. Then, with the car jerking forward as I remember how to work the accelerator, we drive off to school for the Battle of the Bands.

❧

The auditorium has been completely transformed into the closest thing a high school auditorium can be to a dance club. White lights are strung everywhere, silver disco balls and stars hang from the ceiling, and a light machine sweeps multicolored beams around the room. The first several rows of seats have been pulled out and put into storage to create a mosh pit–dance floor area in front of the stage.

Two performance areas are set up, splitting the stage in half, both with drum kits already assembled, speakers, monitors, and amps all in place. All the musicians need to do is plug in and play. While one band is in the spotlight, the next band can get ready for their turn on the darkened half of the stage.

"Whoa, this is awesome," I say.

"Duuuuudes." A deep drawling voice comes from behind us, there's Sam, wearing a black T-shirt with the word *Zildjian* across the front in white letters, his drum brand of choice. Drumsticks stick out of his back jeans pocket.

"Nice set-up, eh?" I ask him.

He sweeps the stage with a sleepy gaze and a slow smile spreads across his face. "Sweet." The guy is so relaxed I wonder if he has a pulse. I wish he could transfer some of his laid-back calm to the girl currently cutting off all circulation to my arm.

"Hey, guys."

I turn, see Ryan, and do a double take. He's wearing tight white pants, a black shirt with a white tie, and shiny black ankle boots. If that wasn't enough, he's got a black fedora pulled down over one eye and sunglasses with red frames. The three of us stare at him, taking this all in, not sure what to say. Then Sam snorts, and we all start to laugh.

"What?" Ryan pulls off his sunglasses.

"Nice outfit," I say.

"Dude, are you wearing makeup?" Sam asks.

"Just a little eyeliner. I borrowed it from my sister. Come on, we're rock stars tonight, why not look like it?" He smiles, punches me in the arm.

"Better to play like one than look like one," I say, punching him back.

"Ah, here they are, Carpe Diem." Ms. Coleman approaches us, clutching a clipboard. She's wearing huge dangly earrings that look like disco balls and a silvery shirt that reflects the colored lights sweeping the auditorium. "There are ten bands playing tonight. You're scheduled here." She jabs a finger at her list, and we circle around to see.

"Next to the last," Sam observes. "That's actually a really good place to be. We'll be fresh in everybody's mind when they do the voting."

"How does that work, anyway? The voting?" I ask.

"It's based on applause," says Ms. Coleman. "At the

end, the bands line up on the stage, and the crowd cheers for their favorite band. The one with the loudest audience response wins a trophy and two hundred dollars."

Ryan and Sam exchange crooked smiles, no doubt imagining a crowd gone wild. Would be nice. But I have my doubts.

Hailey buries her face in my shoulder. "Next to the last," she whispers, and I know what she's thinking. For her, the waiting will be torture. She's got all night to be nervous.

"Make sure you're ready to go on stage at around nine thirty," says Ms. Coleman. Not waiting for a response, she clutches the clipboard to her sparkly shirt and rushes off.

❧

Within the hour, the Thoreau High School auditorium—dance club is rocking with noise and lights and people, and I'm wishing Joey and Matt were here to share this with me. With Joey on drums and Matt on bass and vocals, we would've blown these uptight New England bands out of the water with some of our rocking original songs. Not to brag or anything, but we were pretty damn good. I wonder if Joey's Uncle Phil actually gave our CD to that guy at the House of Blues. I wonder if his record label ever tried to contact us and I screwed things up for everybody by running away.

At about eight thirty, Hailey is in the girl's room. Again. She says she just needs to check on her makeup, but I know she's in there with Danielle and some of her other friends trying to stay calm. I hope it works. Even if her blood sugar is under control, she could psyche herself out so bad that the stage fright could still get her.

The band onstage is this punk group called Snapper, playing a mangled version of a Sex Pistols song. So far, none of the bands have impressed me, so I'm starting to think we might actually have a chance to win some cash. I scan the crowd, and I'm surprised to see familiar faces. Thomas, Suzanne, and Nessa. A grin on my face, I push through the crowd to get to them. I search for Jack too but don't see him.

"Hey, what are you guys doing here?" I shout to be heard over the music.

"You think we'd miss this?" Thomas asks, and he gives me a hug that's more like a pound on the back. "Although this song is causing me actual pain," he admits. "My band used to do it. A whole lot better too."

"I can believe that."

Nessa looks up at me with this shine to her eyes like she thinks I'm amazing, and I won't lie, it makes me feel really good. Dressed in a clean white shirt and jeans, without all that dark makeup she used to wear, she doesn't look anything like a street kid anymore. Just another cute girl at Thoreau High. I don't know how she did it, but Nessa has been able to hold on to a sweetness and innocence in spite of everything that's happened to her. Jack seems to be suffering more than she is.

"I didn't know you played guitar," she says, acting shy with me.

"There's a lot I didn't know either when I was with you guys," I say. "Hey, where's Jack?"

The three of them exchange a furtive look, and nobody says anything. The blush drains from Nessa's face, and she goes pale. Uh-oh. This can't be good.

Suzanne clears her throat and loops an arm in Nessa's. "Come on, girlfriend," she says. "Let's see if we can go get a program." The two of them turn toward the back of the auditorium and work their way through the crowd. Nessa glances anxiously over her shoulder at me.

Thomas stands in front of me, arms folded across his wide chest like he's trying to protect us both. "Jack ran away, Hank."

I must have heard him wrong. "Ran away? What happened?"

"Not long after you left with Hailey, I caught Jack rummaging through my medicine cabinet. He was stealing prescription pills. I think he took some—antibiotics probably—without even knowing what they were."

I bury my face in my hands. "Shit. What did you do?"

"Laid into him, of course. Shouted at him, threatened him a little. Did my best to put the fear of God into him. The kid's a junkie-in-training."

"It's not his fault. It's that guy Magpie who—"

"Look, I've seen what drugs do to people. I was pissed, and I was really hard on the kid. I didn't think he'd take off like that, but I can't say I'm sorry for yelling at him."

"But…how could he leave Nessa behind?"

"Probably the best thing he could do for her. We had a long talk with her after he bolted. She's tired, done with running, and she wants stability. She's going to stay with Suzanne until Monday morning, and we'll talk to somebody in child services. Nessa is stronger than you'd think. She's going to be okay, Hank."

"And what about Jack?"

"That's up to him."

I think about Jack's hands shaking, his bruised cheek, dark circles under his eyes. The guy is probably deep into withdrawal by now. Maybe even sick from taking too many random drugs from Thomas's medicine cabinet.

Thomas gives me a hard pat on the back. "Try not to worry about this right now," he says. "You focus on the music. I'll keep on the lookout for Jack."

Snapper finishes its second cringe-worthy song, and Ms. Coleman grabs a microphone and takes the stage, silver shirt reflecting lights like crazy. "Next up, let's hear it for Red Tide."

The darkened side of the stage is now bathed in light, and the next band launches into a Coldplay song. This group is good, really good. Peering closely at the band members, I recognize the girl with the pink-tipped hair, the lanky lead guitarist with his cap on sideways. It's Cameron's band. I want them to be terrible, want to hate their music, but I can't. The singer is good too, just not as good as Hailey.

"This group is the best so far," Thomas says as they launch into their second song.

I shrug, not wanting to agree, even though he's right. *Yeah, but the lead guitarist is an asshole,* I want to say. When they finish, the crowd goes nuts, hooting and whistling like crazy.

"Well, I should get going for now, look for the rest of my band," I say. "We'll be up in a little while."

"Okay, Hank, good luck. We'll be here," Thomas says, giving me another manly whack on the shoulder. "Don't worry about anything. We'll figure it out."

I head backstage and Cameron is there, basking in the glow of a bunch of people who want to tell him how great he was, so I hang back in the wings, not wanting to deal with him. There's no way in hell I'll offer him any praise. To my surprise though, Hailey goes up to him and gives him a long, warm hug. I fight back an attack of jealousy. After all, she's with me, not him. Right? Well, sort of.

They talk quietly, but within a couple minutes their voices rise and they're arguing. Again.

"But I don't want to drive into the city, Cam," Hailey is saying. "Can't you get somebody else?"

"I tried. I couldn't get anybody else," Cameron says. "Come on, Hailey. You said—"

"I know what I said. And now I'm saying you're stressing me out. Can we talk about this some other time? Seriously, Cam."

"But I need to do this tomorrow, Hailey. We can't talk about it another time."

She doesn't need this tonight of all nights. I walk up behind Hailey and stand there like her bodyguard, glaring at Cameron until he notices me. He gives me a double take through suspicious, squinty eyes.

"Nice shirt," he says.

I glance down. The black T-shirt from Nashville. Crap. I wasn't even thinking when I put the damn thing on.

"Thanks," I say. "I like it too."

"Give it back."

Yeah, like I'm going to whip it off right now and hand it to him. "No."

Hailey stands between the two of us, looks ready to burst into tears. "Stop it, you guys. I can't deal with either of you right now."

Cameron and I cut smoldering looks at each other, but for her sake, I shrug. "Nothing to stop, Hailey. Everything's fine."

She closes her eyes, takes deep breaths to control the tears. "Look, I need to go to the girl's room. Brush my hair. Whatever." She walks away, leaving Cameron and me standing there, glaring at each other.

"Why don't you just leave Hailey alone," I say. A statement, not a question.

"And who are you to tell me that? I've known Hailey since we were in kindergarten."

"Guess that gives you a right to bully her into driving you around like she's your chauffeur."

"I lost my license for that chick," Cameron says. "She owes me."

The next band, comprised entirely of girls with blue

hair and white leather miniskirts, walks by. His gaze drifts to follow them, not that I blame the guy. But I don't take my eyes off Cameron's face.

"Let's take this conversation outside," I say. Not to beat him up, just to talk. That's what I tell myself, anyway.

He nods, leads me to a back door, pushes it open and we're outside in a deserted courtyard. It's a coolish spring night, but crickets are already chirping in the long grass behind the school.

"So what's your deal, Cameron?" I ask, stuffing my hands in my back pockets so I won't hit him. "Are you really that much of an asshole that you want to get Hailey all upset just before she has to perform? You trying to sabotage her and have her mess up like last year just so you can prove some point?"

Cameron flinches, obviously not realizing Hailey told me the whole story, but then he regains his swagger by changing the subject. "Hey, I can prove that's my shirt." He jabs a finger in my face. "My name is sewn into the collar."

I stare at him with a snort of laughter. "Oh yeah? Your mommy sews name tags in all your clothes? Is that what you're saying? So little Cammy won't lose his precious clothes?"

He lunges for me then, tries to pull at the neck of the shirt so he can search for his stupid name tag, but I shove him away with both hands like he doesn't matter. Can't get into a fight, not now, when I'm due to play guitar for Hailey in less than an hour.

Cameron comes at me, fists balled, aiming at my nose, but I dodge him, and he swings at the air. I laugh, which just pisses him off more.

Out of the darkness behind the school comes a raspy shout, and the two of us freeze. "Back off," it says. "Or I'll kill you."

17

A DARK FIGURE LUMBERS OUT OF THE SHADOWS AS PANIC rises in my throat like bile. It's got to be Magpie after all, probably with Watchdog and Ginger backing him up in the weeds behind the school, ready to get their revenge, to kidnap or torture me or just shoot me in the head and be done with it.

"Who the hell are you?" Cameron asks.

"Don't talk," I whisper in a tight voice. God, he's going to get his ass killed, just for being the idiot he is.

The figure shuffles into the light, and with a flash of relief that leaves me weak, I see it's not Magpie or one of his men after all. Jack takes two steps forward, something clutched in his fist. His hand twitches and the streetlights gleam off the metal of a blade.

"Leave Hank alone or I swear I'll cut you," he hisses at Cameron.

All the bravado drains out of Cameron's face, along with the color, leaving him pale and ghostly. "Holy shit." His voice is high like a little girl's.

Good, I'm thinking. Scare the crap out of this weasel. He deserves it. I'll make sure nobody gets hurt, but I might enjoy the show before I intervene. Jack takes another step toward Cameron, knife pointed in the direction of his nose, then suddenly Jack collapses before he can even put out his hands to break his fall, smacking his head on the pavement with a sickening thud. The knife falls out of his hand with a clatter.

I hurry to his side as his crumpled body contracts into a fetal position. "Jack!" Blood trickles out of his hair onto his forehead.

"I don't feel so good, Hank." Then Jack's entire body jerks and convulses and his eyes roll so far back in his head, all I can see is white. I shake him, but it does no good, and then foamy stuff starts bubbling out of his mouth.

"Holy shit," Cameron says again, gaping down at Jack.

Leaning down, I place my ear near Jack's mouth to listen. "Christ, he's not breathing." I reach up and shove Cameron to snap him out of his trance. "Call nine-one-one! Now!"

As Cameron fumbles for his phone, I dredge up a long-ago memory of learning CPR in Boy Scouts. Immediately, I start chest compressions, then wipe the foam off his lips, trying to blow air into his slack, reeking mouth without puking. I have no idea how long I'm doing this when I hear the sirens. Then I see the lights and my own heart stops beating.

Flashing lights. Blue, red, blue, red. Blinding me. Like that day with Rosie. In the intersection. In the car. I close my eyes against the lights, the noise, and Jack's blood. When I open them again, I see the accident all over again. Gray truck getting close, closer, then slamming into us. An explosion of color and terror, shattering glass and grinding metal. Ambulance. Police car. Lights. Blue, red. And my God, so much blood.

Scrambling backward now, away from the lights and sirens and the blood, I find my feet and spin away. *Escape*, the beast snarls in my ear. *Run. Now.*

I turn and run smack into a man in a blue uniform who grasps my upper arms in an iron grip.

"Hold on there, son. You're not going anywhere until we figure out what happened here." I struggle against him, but unable to bolt, my body surrenders and I crumple to the ground near Jack.

From somewhere far away I hear Cameron's voice and

the shouting EMTs, but I'm slipping away, the last forbidden memory detonating within me like I stepped on a land mine.

The gray truck is coming at us, at the passenger door, can't stop in time, trapped in Mom's Toyota with its growling muffler and Rosie inside, thin door of metal and glass not enough to protect her. My world collapses on impact, my forehead smashes into the windshield, breaking glass. Rosie is screaming. Save her. Little blond ballerina in pink is broken. Legs twisted under the crushed front of the car. Bone and torn flesh, one leg is cut and bleeding. The other, somehow, is not there. Broken ballerina, crooked one-legged ballerina in a jewelry box, music tinny and distorted before it grinds to a terrible, silent halt.

❧

"Hey, buddy, can you open your eyes for me?" A stranger's voice. "It's going to be okay. We're taking you and your friend to the hospital."

My eyes fly open to stare at the silhouette of a man in shadows leaning over me, blue and red lights swirling behind him.

"Rather than love, than money, than fame, give me truth which is the true wealth."

Strange. Someone is quoting Thoreau.

"What did he say?"

"*I never found the companion that was so companionable as solitude.*" Then I realize I'm the one quoting Henry, to calm myself, to make space from the memory of the accident, the ballerina, alive but broken.

"*If one advances confidently in the direction of his dreams, and endeavors to live the life which he has imagined, he will meet with a success unexpected in common hours.*"

"What is this kid talking about?"

From somewhere near his left shoulder, I hear Cameron telling another officer. "His name's Hank. I don't know his last name."

"Hank," says a police officer, "Did you take anything tonight that might have made you sick? Have you been drinking?"

Henry's words are beads in a rosary, my desperate prayers. "*The universe is wider than our views of it.*"

"He might have just passed out when he saw what bad shape his friend is in," says an EMT. "He doesn't exhibit signs of drug or alcohol abuse. I think the kid is just in shock."

"*The mass of men lead lives of quiet desperation,*" I whisper, shutting my eyes tight. So sorry, Rosie. Mom. Dad. So sorry. I failed you all. And I will myself to just slip away, just die, in that moment on the ground outside Henry David Thoreau Regional High School. Let me die.

"Not till we have lost the world, do we begin to find ourselves."

Someone wheels a gurney over to where I'm lying on the ground, and the EMTs reach burly arms down, ready to lift me onto it and shoot me off to Emerson Hospital. But no, I can't give in. Waving away their arms, I scramble to my feet. Can't let them take me. It's not time yet. There's that thing I still have to do. What was that again? Hailey. I promised Hailey. Something.

"I'm okay," I say quickly and make my rubber legs hold me up to prove it. "Really, I'm fine."

The cop and the EMTs look at each another. "You need to get checked out at the hospital," the cop says gently.

I shake my head adamantly. I clear my throat and gather my wits. "Is Jack all right?" I finally say.

"He probably will be," the EMT says. "His vital signs are stable now, thanks to you. Do you happen to know what he took?" I tell them everything I know, which isn't a whole lot, about the pills from Magpie and about the prescription drugs he stole from Thomas's medicine cabinet.

"We're going to need to take a statement, so even if you refuse medical care, we need to take you to the station," the cop tells me, then turns to say something into the radio on his shoulder.

"But I have to perform. I need to get inside." I jut a thumb toward the school, indicating the muffled pounding of bass and guitar, the wail of a singer's voice. "I'm probably up next. Can't let my friends down." My voice lacks emotion, a stiff robot version of myself.

The cop pulls off his cap, wipes sweat from his forehead with the sleeve of his jacket, and looks at me doubtfully. "You sure you're up to this? You look like you could collapse any second."

"No, it's cool. I'm fine." But my hands are shaking, and in truth, I wonder how I'll manage to play guitar now. Still, I need to get away from these cops and avoid talking about Jack, which is just going to lead to a can of worms I'm not ready to open. As soon as I tell the police my story, everything will be out, and I'll be done.

"Just give me your name, and we'll talk immediately afterward. Okay?"

"Yes, sir. I'm Hank," I say. "Davidson." He writes this down. Still not ready to be Danny, not yet. When he asks for an address and phone number, I go ahead and give him Thomas's. Can't think of any lie that sounds reasonable. Besides, by the time they come looking for me, it won't matter.

I watch as the EMTs roll Jack's gurney into the ambulance, close the back doors, and drive off, blue and red lights still rolling, making me queasy. I press back the memories of Rosie and the accident, push them far away, and there's nothing more to do. So I turn toward the school in a daze. Hardly feel my own feet shuffling through the gravel or my hand on the cold metal door.

As soon as I enter the back hallway of the school, I'm bombarded with bright lights and amplified music. It's like stepping into another world, unconnected and unaware of what just went down outside. With the loud music coming from the stage, it's unlikely anybody heard the shouts or the sirens. I feel like an alien, stumbling with squinted eyes into a surreal universe where I don't belong.

Ms. Coleman spots me in the hallway and gestures at me like crazy. "Hank, there you are!" she shouts in a shrill voice. "Come on, you're up next!"

She ushers me toward the wings, where Ryan, Sam, and Hailey are standing together waiting for one of the bands on the stage, a heavy metal group, to wrap up. Waiting for me. Panicked looks give way to relief and anger as soon as they see me. Ms. Coleman hands me my guitar, and I stand next to the members of Carpe Diem. I sling the guitar strap over my shoulder and avoid looking at anybody.

"Jesus. About time," Ryan says.

"Hank," says Hailey. She's standing there in her slinky black outfit, trembling hands clutching a plastic water bottle. Afraid, beautiful, angry. "Where the hell have you been?"

"Just…" I gesture vaguely. "Outside."

She squints at me in the muted backstage light. "Oh my God, look at you. You've got dirt on your face. Did you and Cameron get into a fight?" Furious, she yanks a tissue out of her pants pocket, saturates it with water from her bottle, and wipes at my face. I wince as she finds some scraped spots on my nose. "I knew it," she murmurs to herself.

"It's not about Cameron," I tell her.

She reaches into my messy hair, tries to make me look presentable, flicks angry green eyes at me. "Then what happened to you out there?"

"Too much to tell right now," I whisper, and my eyes burn with acid tears.

Hailey finishes finger-combing my hair and looks into my face. I don't know what she sees there, but the anger lifts, replaced by concern. "You okay, Hank?" She presses her red lips together.

I look into her pretty face and find myself unable to lie. "I don't know."

She grabs my hands and squeezes tight. Concern gives way to something deeper and she presses her forehead against mine. "Listen, Hank. When we get out there, pretend it's just us, together in the white room, okay?" she says in a soft, soothing voice. "Just you and me, me and you, making music."

I nod, absorbing her words but unable to respond.

"Okay, Carpe Diem," Ms. Coleman says, practically pushing the four of us onto the stage. "Get out there. You're next."

We walk onto the darkened side of the stage and find our places just as the group on the spotlighted half begins to play. I can't seem to register anything they're doing. Can't identify the music, can't hear progressions or lyrics, my senses paralyzed.

As if in slow motion, I turn my attention to the guitar, Thomas's butterscotch Telecaster, and plug it into the amp. Try to get centered, focus. Can't screw up. Have to push everything else on my mind away. My past, my future. Everything. Put it all in a box, lock it shut and place a beast on guard in front of it. I know how to do that, right?

The group before us finishes their tune, and I'm vaguely aware of applause while I go through the opening chords of "Blackbird" in my head. Come on, I can do this. I know this song in my sleep, even knew it in the strange sleep of amnesia when I didn't know my own name.

The lights come up, and it's time for me to play. The crowd is quiet, expectant, a blur of faces. So many faces waiting for me to do something. Anything. My fingers are cramped, curled like claws above the guitar. Can't play a note. Can't do it. Can't move. A dark wave threatens to take me under.

The crowd is silent, holding its breath. They don't realize it's me who's falling apart in front of them. Instead, they're probably wondering if Hailey's going to have an insulin reaction and pass out again. I imagine Ms. Coleman with her cell phone in hand, ready to dial 9-1-1.

Heart thundering in my ears, I screw my eyes tight, try to concentrate, try to move my frozen fingers and conjure music that won't come. I'm failing Hailey and I can't do a thing about it.

But then, the silence is broken by the sound of a voice. A girl's silky alto voice. At first, I'm so lost in my own head that I don't recognize the voice or the song. But it cuts through my panic and I recognize that it's Hailey. Singing "Blackbird," a cappella, without me. Her voice soars to the rafters, so beautiful.

I'm mesmerized along with the rest of the audience, just listening, until she reaches the end of the first verse. Then, as if they have finally come to life, my fingers relax and start to move. They form chords across the frets, hover above the strings, and then come in perfectly for the intro of the second verse. The music consumes me and the magic takes over at last, transcending my fear.

Hailey joins in and starts singing the second verse like this is exactly how we planned it all along. Whatever fear had a hold on her for the past year has completely loosened its grip. I look over the crowd and see people's astonished faces. See them talking to each other, and I know what they're saying. She's doing it this time. She's doing it. And damn, she's good.

I glance over at Hailey and her eyes say, *you and me, me and you. I knew we could do it.*

We get to the end of the ballad verse, *blackbird fly, into the light of a dark black night*, and then, with an explosive crash of cymbals, the band comes to life and we launch through the song a second time, rocking it hard. Colored lights burst onto the stage with that first crash, and the crowd goes nuts, screaming and whistling and hooting. Hailey wails out the vocals, Sam plays the hell out of the skins, and even Ryan plays almost every note perfectly. By the time we finish, people are on their feet, pumping their arms and shouting.

I glance at Hailey, at her pink cheeks and shining eyes. The girl is glowing, the most beautiful thing I've ever seen in my life. She blows me a kiss and a smile takes up my entire face. I want to capture this amazing moment like a photograph to tuck into my heart and brain forever. Remember every single detail. *Carpe Diem*. Seize the day, this moment. Trap it. Keep it. I wish it would never end.

But it has to. The lights go off on our half of the stage and up on the next band, some folkie guitar-and-fiddle group that assaults my ears. For me, this is the beginning of the end. But what a way to go. What a rush.

Backstage, Sam, Ryan, and I congratulate one another. None of us even care about winning anymore. The fact that we got through it was victory enough.

"I told you losers I could do it," Ryan says to nobody in particular and throws his fedora in the air. Sam snatches it and runs away, making Ryan chase him with a whoop.

"You were incredible," I whisper in Hailey's ear.

"You too," she says and gives me a kiss that almost knocks me over.

God, there's so much I want to tell Hailey. So many lies I need to straighten out. I want to tell her how scared I've been this whole time, how scared I still am, and how much I need her. Tell her how I feel like I've always known her, like maybe we were lovers in a previous life, maybe several past lives. That's how I feel about this girl. But how can I tell her any of this?

Before I get a chance, the final band finishes its two-song folkie set, and all the bands are gathered back on the stage for the voting. In the back of the auditorium, I see a pair of policemen standing by, watching and waiting.

One by one, Ms. Coleman calls out the names of the bands and each group steps forward to stir up the crowd and drum up the highest-decibel support. The loudest response, not surprisingly, comes for Cameron's band. But ours sounds like a strong second.

"And the winner is—Red Tide!" Ms. Coleman announces. Lights go wild, the crowd shrieks, the winning band comes forward for their trophy and check. Cameron throws me a triumphant look, and I give him a cheesy salute in congratulations, which obviously confuses him. Okay, we're not exactly friends, but not enemies either. My time has almost run out and there's no energy left for grudges. At least I know he'll be watching out for Hailey after I'm gone.

Everything else is a blur. Somehow I manage to let Hailey take me by the hand to accept congratulations from her mom and dad and Danielle, who says something flirty in my ear that I can't make out. Somehow I accept pats on the back, people yelling in my ear, "You were incredible!" and random girls giving me hugs. I wish I could enjoy some of this.

But I know that the good stuff is dwindling fast. Soon, everything will be out. The cops are waiting right now to ask me questions. Bad stuff is waiting for me and I can't put it off much longer.

I spot Thomas, Suzanne, and Nessa near the foot of the stage, and the three of them rush forward to congratulate me. They tell me how great the guitar sounded, how our group totally should've won the award, and I make myself smile through it all, dreading what has to happen next. I manage to mumble my thanks, but once they stop gushing and stand there blinking and smiling at me, I don't have it in me to muster one syllable of small talk. I blurt out what has to be said.

"I found Jack outside, behind the school," I tell them. "He's real messed up, but an ambulance came and he's at Emerson Hospital by now. They think he's going to be okay."

Nessa buries her face in her hands and starts to cry, a

mixture of fear and relief. Suzanne puts an arm around her and strokes her hair.

The happy noise of the crowd, people talking and laughing, swirls and bends into a muffled rush of chaos that excludes us. Over there are the normal people of Concord, who have just enjoyed an evening of music and friends and entertainment and safety. And then there's us.

Peering over Suzanne's shoulder, I see two uniformed cops walking toward us. One of them is the guy who took my name. They're waiting to hear my story, to find out how I'm connected to the boy who overdosed behind the high school. This is where the truth comes out, where all the shit in the world hits the fan. After talking to the police, either I'll go home to parents who hate me or straight to jail for my crimes in New York. This is where I say good-bye to Hank forever and have to be Danny Henderson full time again.

But I am still not ready.

Hailey catches my eye from where she stands with her family near the edge of the stage. "Hank, can you come over to the house to celebrate?" she asks. "My mother made a cake and everything."

"I can't, Hailey." I grab her hand, tight, and kiss her fingers. "I have to go."

She blinks at me, green eyes flecked with gold, piercing mine. Seeing me. And I know it's not my imagination. The girl can read me like a book and she can sense the raw finality there, loud and clear.

"You're going?" she whispers in disbelief. "Before you even tell me who you really are?"

My eyes prickle with tears. "I have to," I whisper back. "I'll contact you, I promise. I'll tell you everything." Then I let go of her hand as the cops approach, radios crackling on their hips, handcuffs clinking, badges blinding.

"Oh hey, I forgot the guitar backstage," I say to no one in particular, giving myself a little smack on the forehead, like *oh, what an idiot.* "Look, I'll go get it and be right back."

There are only a few feet between me and the stage. I turn, take the steps two at a time, push my way behind the curtain. I hear Thomas's voice behind me, "Hank, wait," but I ignore it.

The second I'm out of sight, I jog down a long, dark hallway leading away from the auditorium, away from the stage, away from people. As soon as I reach a side door, I open it a crack, and when I'm certain there's nobody lurking outside in the schoolyard or behind the trees, I slip as silently as possible into the shadows.

Sucking cool, fresh air into my lungs, I sprint full speed from the high school grounds, arms and legs pumping, then straining. Blending into the dark night.

Running, again.

18

A DRAGONFLY WITH GREEN EYES LANDS ON MY ARM AND a long-legged spider climbs up the leg of my jeans, but I don't move. Can't scare the moose or let him know I'm hidden behind this spruce tree.

The moose has long spindly legs, a humpback brown body and a goatee. I don't know how he holds those huge antlers up. Leaning over to take a deep drink from the pond, he almost looks harmless, like a horse or something. But I know better. A moose could kick a person to death if he's really pissed.

Ow! A black fly bites the back of my neck, and I smack it, which startles the moose and makes the dragonfly shoot off into the woods. I hate these stupid black flies, and the mosquitoes are just as bad. Last night huddled in my sleeping bag with my flashlight, I counted seventy-two bites. No kidding. Seventy-two. And every one of them still burns and itches.

Hazards on the Appalachian Trail: Biting flies and mosquitoes. I get it now. Though I'd add moose to that list too.

I hold my breath as the moose lifts his huge head to stare at me, pond water dripping off his goatee. If he charges, I'll climb this tree as fast as I can. All the muscles in my body are tense, waiting.

But the moose doesn't charge. He just stands there, looking at me with his black eyes pretty much the same way I'm looking at him. Like I'm incredibly interesting, but he's worried about what I'll do next. When nothing happens on either side, he ducks his head back into the water, yanks up some green pond weeds, and chews calmly, ignoring me.

It's Monday morning, the start of my first full day in the wilds of Maine. The moose sighting is a good omen, I'm sure of it.

Now that I'm in Maine, standing in the woods watching a moose, Saturday night seems like forever ago, a weird dream I had once. But it really happened. After escaping from the high school, I sprinted to Thomas's place to get a backpack, clothes, and all the money I'd saved. From his basement, I grabbed some camping gear and wrote a quick note: "Borrowing some stuff. Promise to bring it back. Thanks for everything."

After taking the last train to Boston, I made my way to South Station, and then caught the first bus in the morning to Bangor. Tried to sleep on the bus, resting my head on the backpack, but that didn't work. My thoughts were crazy, like bees swarming around in my brain. Hailey, Jack, Nessa, and Thomas were all in there with me, along with my parents.

And Rosie. Especially Rosie.

Ever since the accident, I've been on the run, like a voice inside is telling me to keep moving. But there's another voice now, getting louder and harder to push aside.

You really think you can run away from Rosie and what happened to her? Go face your life, the fact that the accident was your fault. Face Rosie. Face Mom and Dad.

I know, I tell the voice. But I can't. Not yet. Let me do this last thing and I'll go back. I promise.

This final leg of my journey feels right on some kind of bone-deep soul level. I followed Thoreau to Concord to find out who I was, and now I'm following Thoreau to Maine. Maybe here I can figure out who I'm supposed to be next. At least this trip will give me a chance to clear my head before surrendering to the mess I left behind.

In Bangor I bought more supplies: a jackknife, waterproof matches, fishing line, and trail food. All those years being a Boy Scout and camping out with my dad definitely came in handy preparing for this trip.

At the Bangor Post Office, I bought one sheet of stationery, one envelope, and one stamp, and then stood at the counter for a long time, trying to write a letter to Hailey.

Dear Hailey,

Wow. I don't know what to say to you. I guess "I'm sorry" would be a good place to start. I'm sorry I wasn't honest with you from day one, but I hope you understand once you hear my whole story. When I first met you, I didn't know who I was. I mean, seriously. I had amnesia, couldn't remember my name, or where I lived, or anything. It wasn't until after I met Thomas (the guy I told you was my uncle) that I finally figured out who I was and why I was such a mess.

My real name is Danny, and I live near Chicago. I ran away from home and lost my memory for a bunch of reasons, but the biggest one is that I was in a car accident where my little sister got hurt really bad. I was the driver. Sure, Thomas keeps telling me it was an accident, but it was still my fault and it tears me apart every minute. Anyway, not looking for sympathy here, just trying to explain so maybe you can understand me better.

I met you and to be honest, for a while I didn't even care who I was. I could almost stop thinking about it all. You made me feel happy, and the music we shared was amazing. Thank you so much for that.

Hailey, I still need to figure some stuff out, but once I do, I'll contact you. I can't stop thinking about you and I want to see you again. Maybe you're really mad at me and don't want to see me at all, but I hope you'll give me a second chance.

Don't know what to say other than I really miss you and I'm sorry.

I stopped and considered how I should close the letter. *Your friend? Sincerely? Take Care? See ya?* But then I decided just to write exactly what I felt:

> *Love,*
> *Hank (Danny)*

From Bangor, I walked or thumbed rides the rest of the way here. The deeper into Maine I traveled, the more natural everything looked. It was honest-to-God wilderness, or as Thoreau called it, "the wild." Found my way to Baxter State Park early last night and set up camp. The only drawback is the bugs, but I bet there's not even one black fly up at the summit of Mount Katahdin.

The moose lifts its big head and peers into the woods, weeds dripping water from his mouth. Voices approach our hiding place. The moose gives me one last glance, then sloshes out of the pond and gallops into the woods, crunching through the underbrush. He disappears within a few seconds.

"I can't believe we're just turning around and going home," says a girl's voice. "Just like that. Giving up."

"Babe, it's way too windy. No need to take the chance," a guy answers. "Look, the mountain will still be there another day."

The two of them come into view, a couple probably in their early twenties, wearing hiking boots and daypacks. They kneel down near the edge of the water. The guy dips his hands in the pond and splashes cool water on the back of his neck.

I wonder what to do. Should I clear my throat to let them know I'm here, maybe say hello? In truth, I don't feel like talking to anybody. So I just stand here behind the tree, feeling like a creepy stalker, watching the girl scoop water onto her face and glare at her boyfriend. Just wanting them to leave.

"It wasn't that bad," the girl murmurs. "We could've made it."

The guy pulls at his sweaty Red Sox T-shirt, takes a deep breath and starts back down the hill, with her close behind. Their voices grow fainter, then disappear into the woods.

Glancing up at the sky through the spruce branches, everything looks clear and blue to me. No doubt things are windier farther up the mountain, but it's going to take some serious weather to discourage me. I'm not sure what I hope to achieve by reaching the top of the mountain, only that I have to get there.

Pulling my backpack up onto my shoulders, I continue hiking uphill. Destination: Baxter Peak, the summit of Mount Katahdin at 5,226 feet above sea level. I can't take the exact route Henry traveled because he did a lot of canoeing and portaging once he got to the wild and I don't have a canoe. But that doesn't matter. What's important is that I'm here, seeing the same landscape he saw, pretty much the way it looked back in the mid-1800s.

And just like Henry, I have the same destination: the

mountain's summit. Except Henry never quite made it. He climbed to South Peak, the second highest peak, and even though that's way impressive, let's face it, it's still not the top. My goal is to get there for both of us.

Hiking up the side of the mountain, I get a good rhythm going, breathing hard but making good progress. The incline is sharp, a wooded path through trees and bushes and over random rock formations. So far, so good. Conditions are still great as far as I can tell, not a lot of clouds. That's important when you're climbing up to where the clouds live.

Focused on steady walking and breathing, my brain clears and I'm able to relax and think like when I settle into the cadence of a good run. And as soon as I do, my thoughts fall into that last black hole of time I couldn't recover, until now. Listening to the pace of my own feet crunching on rocks while climbing the mountain, I'm able in a semi-detached way to examine the missing moments and days right after the accident.

🌿

When my forehead smashed into the windshield, I got a concussion. Brain sloshing against my skull knocked me out, but not for long. Not long enough.

I was aware of people rushing to the car window, saying hang in there, that the ambulance was coming, that it was going to be okay. But it wasn't. At first, Rosie wailed and whimpered like a baby animal caught in a trap, but then she went silent with her blue eyes wide and empty, and that was worse. My head hurt so bad and everything was blurry and I couldn't get to her, couldn't help get her free. Somebody outside the passenger window gasped and said, "Her leg. My God, her leg," and I had to look. But after one quick glance at the place where her leg was supposed to be, I couldn't grasp the sight of blood and bone. My brain locked into wondering, what happened to that other pink sneaker? Where did it go? As soon as I get out of this car, I have to find it.

The ambulance arrived and I can still see the lights flashing, hear my sister screaming while they tried to free her from the wreck. I kept telling them I had to go out there in the road to find the sneaker, but they kept telling me hush, that I was going to be okay. They didn't understand. The trip to the hospital is a blur, and for the next couple of days I guess I swam in and out of consciousness while my brain did its best to recover.

Flashes of memory: bandage on my head, IV drip in my arm, my parents coming to see me, Mom crying. It runs together, those days in the hospital. Sleeping for hours and eating meals brought on a tray, watching TV shows with my eyes glazed over, barely registering what I saw. Then, about the third day after the accident, Mom came to see me and when the doctor came in, he told us I could go home.

As soon as the gauzy haze in my head started to lift, it was all too clear what had happened to Rosie. Her leg was so badly mangled in the wreckage, they couldn't save it. One legged, broken ballerina. Even after I was better, I stayed in my bed all day, every day, refusing to go to school, pretending my head still hurt more than it actually did. Couldn't face the idea of what happened to my baby sister. What I did to her.

Finally, I couldn't stand living inside my own body, couldn't deal with the guilt. I knew I either had to run or I would end up hanging myself in the garage. It was that simple.

So I threw some stuff in a gym bag, emptied my savings account, and got ready to run to New York City, the biggest, baddest place I could think of. I was prepared to vanish into the crowds and somehow cease to exist. Disappear off the grid.

Before I left, I stopped at the hospital to see Rosie. She was out of ICU now, in a private room. Slowly, like I was walking into a cathedral or something, I stepped into her room and stood by her bed. She looked so little in that hospital bed, with one leg and foot molded by the sheets. The other side was flat from the thigh down. Nothing there.

"Rosie," I whispered.

Her eyes fluttered open, and she looked at me, my blond sister with pink cheeks and blue eyes like a little china doll. She smiled. I couldn't believe it. She actually smiled at me. "Danny," she said. Her voice was all sleepy and dreamy, and I'm sure they'd been giving her a ton of drugs, so she wasn't fully aware of her situation. Or whose fault it was.

"I'm so sorry, Rosie," I said. And in that moment, I wanted so badly for her to say something typically Rosie-ish like, *hey Danny, bet you didn't know that the magnolia is both the state flower and the state tree of Mississippi, did you?*

But she was asleep.

I left the hospital with my gym bag slung over my shoulder and caught the train in downtown Naperville that took me to Chicago. From Chicago, all the way to New York City.

My head was pounding the whole way on the train. Not fully recovered from the accident, the concussion, the shock of everything, I slept most of the way, sometimes not even remembering where I was or why I was there. It was dark when I got off the train in New York and sometime within the first few hours of my arrival, I got mugged. All I remember is tripping in a mud puddle as some guy on the street hit me, stole my gym bag and all my money except for a ten dollar bill stuffed in my front pocket. The blow, plus the concussion, added to the trauma of the accident. It all worked together to shut off access to my past. It was self-preservation, guarded by a snarling beast that turned out to be a blessing in disguise. For a while, anyway.

❧

After about an hour, the path becomes steeper, and it's harder to catch my breath. My thigh muscles burn and the backpack, stuffed with my gear, feels heavier with every step. Sitting on a rock, I pull sweaty arms out of the pack and stretch my muscles. The wind is picking up, so I pull out a windbreaker and slip it over my head. There's no way I'm going to be able to carry the pack to the summit. So I pull out a few things and stuff them into my pockets: water bottle, trail mix, flashlight. My book. Then I find a nook under a ledge of granite, and stuff the pack into it, camouflaging it with leaves and pine branches. To make sure I remember where I left it, I tie a white sock on a branch near the path.

It's around noon when a park ranger heading downhill meets me on the trail. I register a gray-beige shirt and brown shorts, a straw-colored hat. "The wind is getting fierce up there," he tells me. "We haven't closed down the summit yet, but we probably will. You might want to turn around and try this another day."

He's a nondescript looking guy. Hair the color of his shirt. Eyes the color of his shorts. It all blends together into a gray-brown blur. "Thanks," I say, "for letting me know."

The ranger considers this, taking in the fact that I'm still standing there and have made no move to retreat. But there's not much he can do. "Just…respect the mountain," he says.

"I will," I tell him. "I do."

He nods at me and continues down the mountain. His job is done. The burden of risk is on me. And that's exactly how I want it.

As I climb higher, the wind moans like a live thing in the pine and oak trees, throws my hair in my eyes. The landscape changes from trees, bushes, and other leafy plants to thin tufts of grass and carpets of moss. The only trees now are small and stumpy, holding on to the windswept ground for dear life.

Every few feet I stop to take in the view, feeling like I'm climbing up into the sky. Far below, trees, lakes, and streams spread out below me like a topographical map from geography class. But the higher I climb, the more the world I know falls away around me, along with the security of trees and foliage, and it's like I'm on some strange alien planet.

Step by step by step, the air gets thinner and there are fewer trees, even the stumpy ones. There's not even much in the way of moss. Just lichen growing like mold on the rocks, green, black, and gray. They're the only living things that won't get blown off the mountain by the wind, surviving because they pretend to be part of the rock.

My windbreaker snaps in the wind like a flag on the mast of a ship. This feels like hurricane wind, tornado wind. An angry wind strong enough to shove me off a mountain.

Just ahead of me lies Knife Edge, which connects Pamola Peak—named after the Native American storm god who supposedly lives on this mountain—with Baxter Peak, the true summit. This is the most dangerous part of this trek. For about a mile, there's this narrow band of rocks, barely two feet wide. I've read about this place. People have fallen off Knife Edge and plummeted 2,000 feet to their deaths. Probably on windy days just like this one.

If I stay low, close to the rocks, I bet I can make it in spite of the wind. My first step falls on loose rocks and I slip, grabbing onto a boulder to steady myself. Adrenaline surges through my body as I hunker down low. On one side, there's a sheer drop. The other side is the same. All that is holding me up on this planet is a narrow strip of rock that I'll have to climb across on all fours in a heavy wind. Yes, I could turn around and try tomorrow. But the summit is there within sight, so close. I'm going to do this.

Halfway across Knife Edge, a crowd of dark clouds drifts in from the other side of the mountain. Instantly, the sun is hidden by clouds and the entire world turns gray. The first drops of rain fall, huge and dense, and the wind begins a low howl.

Stuck in the middle of this precarious strip of land, I cling to a flat boulder like a tiny barnacle in a raging sea. Pressing my head to my chest, I ignore the rock scraping skin off my nose, the dirt and lichen lodged under my fingernails. Can't move forward, can't move back. Stuck, in limbo, within sight of the summit of Mount Katahdin.

So this is it. I've run as far as I can go. Ran away from the flat prairie land of Illinois to New York City and to Concord, Massachusetts. Ran away from my parents and away from Magpie. Mostly, I've tried to run away from what I did. But it follows me wherever I go, even followed me to the top of this mountain. The rain comes harder now, pelting my skin like buckshot.

My sister will never dance again. Hell, she'll never walk again. Not without a fake leg taking the place of the one she lost. How can I climb back down this mountain and go on living with that forever at the core of me? Such a coward, all I could do was run away on my two good legs. God, I can't think about this. But I can't run either. Not this time. I'm trapped here with myself and my thoughts.

Wind and rain slap my face, whip across my back, my arms, my legs. The shrieking could be the howling of the wind, or it could be me. Salt tears and fresh rainwater stream down my face, into my mouth. How can I ever go home again?

A new realization breaks over me. Truth is, I don't have to go home. Don't have to face my parents. Don't have to feel pain anymore. All I have to do is let go of this rock. Stand up, throw my arms out to the sky, and let the wind take me. This, here and now, could be my fate. This would be a clean ending to my useless life. A good way to die.

Slowly, I peel shaking fingers off the rock, imagine the release as I let the wind shove me off the mountain, imagine falling like flying, sweet relief. I tense the burning muscles of my legs, ready to stand. To surrender.

No, Danny.

A voice rides the wind.

I lift my head up and squint against the wind and rain, somehow expecting Rosie to be here next to me, clinging to this rock, blond angel in pink. The voice is that clear, that familiar. But nobody is here. I duck my head back down.

No, boy, don't do it.

This time it's Henry's voice, carried by a fresh gust of wind. "Where are you?" I cry out.

Can't see Rosie, can't see Thoreau. I'm alone, peeling myself off a rock on a mountain, about to die. But the voices come again, inside my head.

Danny, hold on. You have to hold on. This time it's Cole, or at least the essence of the little brother who died too soon.

"I don't know how to do this, Cole," I yell into the storm. "I couldn't save you, couldn't protect Rosie. I can't do this anymore."

Choosing life means facing pain and I'm just not strong enough. Death is the final, ultimate escape for those of us who run. So it has come to this: hold on to the rock and live. Or let go and die.

Think of Mom and Dad. It would kill them, and they've been through enough. Don't you see? It's both Rosie and Cole now, arguing in my head together, double-teaming. *You're no coward, Danny.*

Yes, I am. I'm the one who runs away.

The wind slaps at me like a heavy hand. It hurts and I want it to hurt. I deserve it. It tears my wailing voice away. It would be easy, so easy to let go.

I wanted to live deep and suck out all the marrow of life…to put to rout all that was not life…and not, when I came to die, discover that I had not lived. Henry's voice in my head, so real I almost expect to see his face floating in front of me.

No, Henry, I haven't lived. Not really. But I'm done, don't you see? Can't suck out the marrow of life when I'm too afraid to live. Too broken.

Every creature is better alive than dead, men and moose and pine trees, and he who understands it aright will rather preserve its life than destroy it.

Another Henry-ism. Damn you, Henry.

If I decide to live, all I have waiting for me is a broken family and no idea of what to do with the rest of my life. What do I do with that?

Clinging to a rock in a violent rainstorm, there's nowhere left for me to run, nothing left to do. The thing I want most is to hurl myself into permanent forgetful-ness. But for the sake of the voices in my head, I hesitate. I force myself to imagine a life past this moment.

Finishing high school. I could do that. Can't see myself going to college, not now anyway, but maybe I'd work at a music shop for a while. Learn how to repair guitars. Maybe I could even go back to Concord. Be with Hailey and work with Thomas.

But what about my family? Can't keep my parents from splitting up, but maybe we could finally talk about Cole. That would be a start.

The wind is just beginning to quiet down when I force myself at last to think of Rosie. Make myself imagine Rosie in a wheelchair, Rosie learning to walk with an arti-ficial leg. Maybe if she forgave me for the accident, I could help her. Be there for her like we always were when things in our family came apart.

Whether it's the essence of Rosie, Cole, Henry, or something wise beyond understanding inside myself, I don't know. But finally, it gets through to me. I can't die leaving behind the mess that Danny created. And as long as I have life, there's hope I can live better, find a way to be the best of Danny, plus Hank. For Rosie, for my parents. For myself.

I don't know how long I lie there holding on to the

rock, letting the rain drench my hair, my clothes, my skin, but finally the clouds drift off toward the horizon, and the storm retreats.

Hands cramping, knees clutching, everything hurts, but I start crawling forward again. Keep going, listening to the voices in my head that insist I live. Closer and closer to the other side of Knife Edge. When it's safe, I stand up, stretch sore limbs, take a few steps. Walk toward Baxter Peak, the summit of Mount Katahdin.

Nobody is here but me to see the world cracked open, to look out on the world and see hundreds of miles into the distance, to smell the rain-cleansed air. Somehow, I feel clean too.

I stumble over to the weathered brown sign that reads KATAHDIN and under that in smaller letters, BAXTER PEAK, NORTHERN TERMINUS OF THE APPALACHIAN TRAIL.

After reading this, I shake my head, thinking of my dad, not sure if I should laugh or cry. *Look at me, Dad. I reached the end of the Appalachian Trail before you and I never saw the beginning.*

Touching the rough wood with both hands, I gather strength from its solidness. Then I reach into the back waistband of my jeans and pull out the book.

You know where to find me, Henry had said. And it's true, I do. He's at Walden Pond. He's here in Maine. He's anywhere nature has the power to make me stop and think. And most of all, he's in this book.

Walden is in worse shape than when I found it on the floor at Penn Station those long weeks ago. Now it's drenched by the mountain storm. Pages are bent over and torn, and some are missing—the ones Frankie ate and the ones that fell out because I carried it around and thumbed through it so often. I don't know for sure if it was always mine or if some traveler left it at the train station, but that doesn't matter now. Thoreau brought me here. I may not be Thoreau reincarnated, but I bet I could live the rest of my life as if I were. Living an authentic, simple life makes a whole lot of sense to me.

And there's one more thing. If I was Thoreau reincarnated, I bet he would've wanted me to complete something he couldn't in his own lifetime: reach the true summit of Mount Katahdin. So here I am, for both of us.

I set *Walden* at the base of the sign like a sacred offering to the gods. Then I take from my pocket the smooth white stone I brought from Walden Pond, and set it on top of the book to keep it anchored.

"There you go, Henry," I say. "You made it."

I stand there for a long time. Then I turn to walk back down the mountain.

Luckily there's more than one route to and from the summit, so I decide to avoid Knife Edge this time by choosing a different path down the mountain. I've walked only a few minutes when I spot a man with a crooked walking stick about fifty feet below me and heading my way. He pauses to take off his straw hat and wipe rain and sweat off his forehead with a red bandana. Something about the way he stands, his black goatee and muscular build, look familiar.

The man looks up at me, shields his eyes against the sun, and waves, the bandana like a banner in his hand.

I wave back in disbelief. "Thomas," I call out, and I start to laugh. "What are you doing here?"

But of course I know what he's doing here. It wouldn't take much for a research librarian–historian to figure out where I was going when I left Concord. After all, he planted the idea in my head to begin with. And now, he has come to find me.

"Dan!" he shouts back. At first I'm startled to hear him use my real name, and Dan instead of Danny, but it's okay somehow. In fact, I like it. When I climbed up the mountain this morning, I was still Hank. I'm not Hank anymore. But in truth, I'm not Danny either. For good or for bad, I'll be Dan Henderson from now on. New name, fresh start.

I'm so busy smiling like a goofball and lumbering down the mountain toward Thomas, I almost trip on an outcropping of granite in the middle of the path. By the time I recover and look back to where Thomas waits, there's another man standing behind him.

It's a tall man wearing shorts and hiking boots with black shaggy hair poking out from under a baseball cap. I can see the logo from here. The Chicago Cubs. We both stand there, frozen, allowing this stunning reality to break over us.

"Dad?"

"Danny." My father speaks my name, his voice lifted to my ears by the same wind that nearly pushed me off the mountain. I hold the moment like it's a paper-winged butterfly, unable to believe the fragile truth of it.

Gravity pulls me down the mountain path, to the place where my father stands and waits, his arms open wide.

I collapse against my father's chest and he squeezes the breath out of me with his strong arms. He came all this way to find me. Maybe I can be forgiven after all. I can hardly stand up with the relief of this. His arms hold me on my feet when I want to fall and kiss the magic ground.

Dad looks me over with his hands on my shoulders like he's convincing himself it really is me there in front of him, and all in one piece. "Danny," he says again, choking on my name. And then he crushes me to himself all over again like it will help him believe.

When I pull back and peer into his eyes, I can't say her name, can't ask. But of course, he knows.

"Rosie's going to be okay," he says. "She's a strong little girl. But she needs her big brother."

Inside me somewhere, the beast shrinks and contracts into itself until it is nothing but pure white light.

"All she wants—all any of us want—is for you to come home."

Home.

I drink the word like someone who has been lost in the desert without water for more days than I can count and gulp it down.

Dad takes a tissue out of his back pocket and blows his nose into it with his signature honk. He stuffs it into his pocket and turns to Thomas, who is standing at a polite distance trying not to look like he's eavesdropping as he rubs at his own watering eyes.

"But first, Thomas, there's no way we're going to get this close and not stand at the summit of Mount Katahdin."

Thomas grins at us both. "Well, hell yeah. I've always wanted to set foot on the official ending of the Appalachian Trail."

"The ending." Dad echoes and looks at me. We lock eyes, and I know exactly what he's thinking. What looks like the ending could just as easily be considered the beginning.

That's when the last words Henry wrote in *Walden* pop into my head. And I realize the ending of *Walden* isn't really an ending either.

Only that day dawns to which we are awake. There is more day to dawn. The sun is but a morning star.

Dad smiles, pats me on the back, and together with Thomas we turn toward Baxter Peak and the huge blue-gray sky above us and walk.

Acknowledgments

So many people to thank, so many things to say, so much love to spread around. Borrowing a line from my favorite book-turned-movie, *The Princess Bride*: "There is too much—let me sum up."

Thank you…

…first and foremost, to Lesléa Newman, friend, teacher, mentor, author, and literary cheerleader extraordinaire.

…to editor Wendy McClure, for "having a feeling" about my book, and agent Rubin Pfeffer who said, "this should be your debut novel—when can I see the rest?"

…to Cal's Marketing Team (CMT), Tedford and (future published author) Nicolle, for supporting me and helping do the things I suck at doing, which is a lot. And to mini-me Cori for loving and supporting all of us.

…to the best writing group buddies ever: Pauline Briere, Pam McKinney, Amy Safford, Kara Storti, Chris Daly, Karen Jersild, and Meriah Crawford.

…to the fabulous instructors/mentors from the Stonecoast MFA program at the University of Southern

Maine, especially: Brad Barkley, Suzanne Strempek-Shea, and Elizabeth Searle.

...to Richard Smith, the real-life tattooed Thoreau interpreter/historian/punk rocker/rebel who was my Henry fact-checker and helped solidify the character of Thomas.

...to the amazing people who have shared (and continue to share) the magic of music in my life...you know who you are...

...and to Edmund and Ruth Anne Claypool who provided me with a lifetime supply of love and encouragement (not to mention art and writing supplies). Thanks, Mom and Dad.